Time's Passage

Time's Passage

Marcia Amidon Lusted

Marcia Amidon Lusted
2001

Writers Club Press
San Jose New York Lincoln Shanghai

Time's Passage

Writers Club Press
an imprint of iUniverse.com, Inc.

For information address:
iUniverse.com, Inc.
620 North 48th Street, Suite 201
Lincoln, NE 68504-3467
www.iuniverse.com

ISBN: 0-595-13882-9

Printed in the United States of America

To Greg,

my husband and best friend

CHAPTER 1

The metallic clatter of the warning bell cut through the noise of conversation in the halls, and everyone began moving lethargically toward homeroom. Lindsay made one last attempt to comb her hair into something less boring than usual, then gave up, and slammed her locker door shut in disgust. It was only the first week of October, but she already felt like she'd been in tenth grade for about a thousand years, and here was yet another endless day. Hoisting her books higher in her arms, she plunged into the general shuffle.

Suddenly something caught her eye as she passed by the Drama Club bulletin board. AUDITIONS FOR CAMELOT, a notice screamed at her, THIS YEAR'S FALL PRODUCTION. SIGN UP NOW!

Camelot. The mythical kingdom of King Arthur. For a moment Lindsay was actually tempted to audition, remembering the stories she'd read when she was younger, and the movie her mom had rented once. On stage, she could be gorgeously costumed as a lady-in-waiting…singing and dancing gracefully for an audience of hundreds of people. With a sigh, Lindsay felt her terminal shyness reassert itself, and if that wasn't enough to quench her theatrical ambitions, then she saw her sister Kathi's name on the sign-up sheet.

Kathi was a senior this year. That really said it all, but she was also as different from Lindsay as two sisters raised by the same parents could possibly be. She was social where Lindsay was academic, only pulling in

B's and C's to Lindsay's usual A's, but she had always had a boyfriend since the third grade and had been in just about every club the school sponsored, with the possible exception of Chess and Computers, although maybe that was just from lack of time. What was often even harder to deal with was that Kathi was honestly and completely nice. Unlike their other sister Andrea, Kathi never had that typical older sister mean streak, and had honestly tried to help Lindsay settle into high school. No matter how much she wanted to, Lindsay just couldn't dislike her for being pretty and popular.

With a wistful sigh, Lindsay turned away from the bulletin board. Kathi was a devoted member of the drama club, and Lindsay just knew she'd get the part of Guinever. Nothing on earth would convince Lindsay to stand on the same stage, shy and awkward, where everyone knew she was Kathi's sister and felt sorry for her. Lindsay made her way into homeroom just as the tardy bell rang, sliding into her seat and dropping her books on the desk with a thump.

"Lindsay!" Her best friend, Chris Harris, extricated herself from a huddle of girls who were probably discussing boys, judging from the volume of giggles and squeals. "I thought you'd never get here!" She sat down in the next chair. "Did you see the Drama board? Are you going to audition? I am! Will Kathi get the lead?"

Chris had to stop here to take a breath, and Lindsay had to grin at her enthusiasm. They'd been friends since alphabetical order first threw them together in second grade. Back then they hadn't cared about much except books and creating fantasy worlds in Chris's tree house. Chris was pretty in a haphazard sort of way, being blonde and green-eyed and slim, but until recently she'd had a total lack of interest in her appearance. This year, however, she suddenly seemed to be transforming before Lindsay's eyes into one of those alien, effervescent girls that both of them used to envy and disdain. But they were still best friends, even if Chris sometimes seemed more interested in Kathi's company these days, and their loyalty to each other went a long way.

Chris was looking expectant, so Lindsay grimaced and said, "Kathi's a sure thing to be Guinever." She attempted to sound bored.

"So? That doesn't mean you can't audition…Mrs. Cummings just loves underclassman, and with Kathi as your sister, it should be easy!"

Chris's cheerfulness was irritating. "That's exactly why I don't want to try out!" Lindsay snapped.

Chris looked at her as if she had suddenly gone insane, but the morning announcements came over the PA system before she could open her mouth again. She had to carry the argument out to the hall and into first period English.

Miss Pace was explaining relative pronouns with great relish, and Lindsay occupied herself by drawing wandering graffiti in the margins of her notebook. Sam Carter, in the seat behind her, suddenly jabbed her in the back and flipped an elaborately folded note onto her desk. Chris, no doubt. After a quick glance at Miss Pace, who was still safely wrapped up in her pronouns, Lindsay carefully smoothed out the note on her lap:

Lindsay!
You HAVE to audition!
I can't do it alone…I need
moral support!
-C-
(P.S.—Don'tcha think Sam's cute?)

Lindsay sighed, thinking that Chris wrote in exactly the same style of punctuation that she spoke with…all exclamation points and no full stops. She also seemed to be switching into high gear as far as being on the lookout for any budding social possibilities. She's going to leave me aimlessly drifting in perpetual adolescent turmoil, Lindsay thought, and was rather pleased with the drama of that statement.

She wrote back on the bottom of the note:

> I really DO NOT want to try out and I AM NOT changing my mind.
> And yeah, Sam's cute, but he also knows it.
> -L-

Lindsay carefully refolded the note and dropped it back over her shoulder, where it was neatly intercepted by Miss Pace and subsequently read aloud to the entire class. Lindsay had always considered that teacher's trick to be particularly insensitive and unfair. By the time the bell rang, her face was flaming and Sam was thinking that she was a snob and a jerk. But he did stop to talk to Chris.

Chris caught up with Lindsay in the hall and made soothing noises about the beastliness of teachers in general and Miss Pace in particular.

"I won't mention the fact that it was all your fault," Lindsay said, pointedly.

Chris ignored that, returning relentlessly to the subject of "Camelot".

"Won't you at least try, Lin?" she wheedled, "I know you can sing, I've had to listen to you singing with the radio for years! You can act, too…remember all those stories we used to do in the treehouse? I bet you'd do great on stage!" She said this in such a maternal, encouraging way, as if coaxing a little kid, that Lindsay wanted to slap her.

"I don't want to take away from Kathi's spotlight," she told Chris loftily, "It's her last year. She doesn't need me tagging along after her. Besides, you know perfectly well that I can't stand up there, singing and dancing in front of strangers."

Chris looked disappointed, but apparently decided to admit defeat and give up on the argument. Lindsay was curious as to why Chris wanted her moral support so much anyway…lately she'd been doing all sorts of things on her own, without Lin. She was probably still insecure about some of the new social territory she was treading.

"Oh, well," Chris sighed, "I'm still going to audition. I've always wanted to be in a real show, not just the freshman class play like last year." She paused outside the door of her science class and added, "Will you at least come to the auditorium tomorrow and sit with me? Just for company?"

Lindsay looked at her friend's pleading expression and relented a little. She shrugged and grinned.

"Okay." she said, "But just for company."

Chris gave her a real Chris grin, the kind she hadn't seen in a while, and squeezed her arm. "Thanks, Lin! See you at lunch!"

She disappeared and Lindsay continued on down the hall, feeling vaguely depressed. It was a lonely feeling, knowing that she and Chris were drifting apart, and it was even lonelier to know that Chris felt sorry for her. It was enough to really spoil her day.

CHAPTER 2

The bus left Lindsay off at the corner as usual, and she took her time walking up to the house. It was a perfect October afternoon, with a warm golden light and the smell of wood smoke. She scuffed lazily through piles of fallen leaves to the kitchen door, which still had its summer screen. It banged very satisfactorily behind her.

No one else was home yet. Lindsay dumped her books in the big chair by the fireplace and went to rummage in the refrigerator for a snack. Last night's pie was tempting and she eyed it, speculatively, but there was her extra twenty or so pounds to consider. But after a day like today...The pie won out, and she cut herself a big hunk.

Returning to the comfy chairs by the fireplace, Lindsay plunked herself down and flipped on the television. The afternoon talk shows were on, as usual, so Lin decided to see what they were up to today. It took a few minutes and several commercials before she got the gist of one: the oddly dressed assortment of guests was all supposedly psychics.

Instantly Lindsay's stomach began to roll and she clicked off the TV and went over to the window. She pressed her forehead against the cool glass and watched a mother passing by with two little kids in a stroller. Lindsay closed her eyes and concentrated for a moment: the woman was thinking, regretfully, that she would give just about anything to be back at college in the fall, with her whole life ahead of her, instead of here...Lin shook her head and turned off the rest.

That was the truth of it. She was a freak, just like those oddballs on the talk show, because with a little effort she could tell what many people were thinking, in little glimmers and flashes, or even complete thoughts, if the emotion was strong enough. Lindsay had been denying this talent for as long as she could remember, hoping it would go away from disuse, but it was like riding a bike: you never forgot how. And it was always catching her unawares.

Wandering distractedly back to her chair, Lindsay toyed with the piece of pie and then decided she didn't want it after all. She carried it back to the kitchen sink and scraped it down the disposal, then saw her mom's car pull in. She had never told anyone, not her parents or her friends or anyone, that she thought she was telepathic. She would never run the risk of being labeled a freak, even in the best interests of science or something.

"Hi, honey!" her mother called out cheerily, as she banged open the door from the garage, "Help me with these groceries, will you?"

"Hi, Mom," Lindsay answered, and went out to the car to grab some bags. As she came back in, her mom gave her a highly scented kiss on the cheek. She was dressed up, just back from showing a house to some prospective buyer.

"Sell anything today?" Lindsay inquired, a bit flippantly, trying to feel normal again after the talk show scare. "If you did, you'd be way ahead of Dad this month." Her father sold cars, and the two of them had an informal contest as to who was the best salesperson in any given month.

"Perhaps," her mom replied, smiling as always, "The Tuckers just loved the MacPherson place, but they want to check a few other houses before they decide. How was your day?"

"Okay," Lindsay replied tersely, and her mother wisely did not pursue it any further. School hadn't been the high point of Lindsay's day for approximately six years or so.

"There's a letter from Aunt Sam in my purse," her mother called from the pantry, and Lindsay perked up. Rummaging around in her mom's huge pocketbook, she found a thick packet with British stamps. She snatched it up and carried it off to her chair like a prize.

Aunt Sam was really Samantha, of course, and her mom's little sister, as well as Samantha Ellerton, the noted scholar in medieval history. She'd been living in England for the past ten years, and Lindsay thought with a giggle that she was so thoroughly English now, accent and all, that you'd never guess she was born in Massachusetts. Lindsay slit open the letter with her finger and got a paper cut for her pains. Sucking away the blood, she read it eagerly.

"What does she have to say?" her mother inquired, from the vicinity of the stove.

"She's got a new archeological sight in Cornwall," Lindsay replied, turning a page, "She's renting a flat there for six months or so…Hey, maybe you can send me over there to be her assistant?"

"I don't think so," her mom said, lightly, "After all, you have a little thing called school. What else?"

"The usual," Lindsay said, bringing the letter back, "Stuff you'd be interested in…she's been putting up with the usual tourist relatives who need a free place to stay. When can we go over there again?"

"When I sell about twenty more houses," Mom replied wryly, "Now help me get supper. Where's your sister?" She said this as if she had suddenly remembered Kathi's existence. Lindsay's other sister, Andrea, had just gone off to college, and Lin thought privately that her absence had just confused Mom even more, leaving her with a perpetual feeling of someone unaccounted for.

"The Drama Club starts auditions for the fall play," Lindsay said, getting out salad ingredients, "She's probably in a huddle with Mrs. Cummings, the director. I think Kathi's going to get the female lead."

"What's the show?"

"Camelot."

"Camelot?" Mom suddenly paused, and smiled almost dreamily. "We did that show in college. I was dating the guy who played King Arthur… It's a wonderful show. Do you know it?"

Lindsay shrugged noncommittally. "I know the King Arthur stories. Chris is all excited about it. She wants to get a part." Instantly she wanted to kick herself for mentioning it.

"Chris is auditioning?" her mother remarked, too brightly. "Hmm. Lin, why don't you join her? It would be great fun, and with Kathi there the three of you could have a wonderful time."

Lindsay clamped her lips together tightly and said nothing. It would only lead to the old "get involved" speech again, and she could never possibly explain to her mother why it was imperative to keep a low profile, always. Being noticed, being "involved", could only lead to a slip-up, which would expose Lindsay as a freak, ready for the next episode of the X Files.

"I'm not interested." she told her mother brusquely, and was rewarded with the usual half-hurt, half-exasperated look that she knew so well.

"Lindsay," her mother began, "being involved in activities would help you make new friends, gather new interests, and it would look good on those college applications…"

"Forget it!" Lindsay interrupted her angrily. "I'm never going to be popular like Kathi and Andrea, and you might as well face it now! I'm just the family dud!" She ran out of the room and thudded up the stairs. Moments later her door slammed.

Lindsay's mother sighed, and returned to her cooking with a thoughtful look. She had always let Lindsay off the hook when it came to not forcing her into things she didn't want to do, but she seemed to be more withdrawn every year. Perhaps it was time to force the issue a little.

Upstairs in her room, Lindsay flopped down on her bed angrily. She heard Kathi come clattering in from the late bus and then the deep rumble of her father's voice when he came home. Pretty soon Kathi chirped at her to come to supper, and she had no choice but to go down and face the issue again. She knew, of course, that her mother wasn't going to let it drop this time.

CHAPTER 3

Lindsay crept to the dinner table. Kathi was already eating, chattering madly at the same time.

"The show this year is going to be wonderful!" she gushed, while spearing pieces of chicken with her fork. "We're all set for auditions tomorrow. You're going to come, aren't you, Lin? I'm so glad you're finally old enough to do a show with me before I graduate."

Lindsay groaned audibly while her mother shot a triumphant glance at her father.

"What a great idea, Kathi!" she said cheerfully.

"I told Mrs. Cummings about you, and she'll be watching for you," Kathi continued.

"Kathi…" Lindsay said, through clenched teeth, "I can't audition for the play. I'd rather die first."

"Oh, come on, it's not that tough!" Kathi replied, unquenched, "Everyone gets cold feet, but once it's over you'll wonder why you were nervous."

"Nervousness is good," their father added, succinctly, "Builds character."

"Oh, Dad," Kathi said, rolling her eyes, "So anyway, Lin, meet me in the auditorium after school and I'll introduce you around."

Lindsay felt panicked, like a trapped animal. Kathi was trying so hard, and was so hopeful, but…

"Kathi, I can't!" she said, with a rising note of hysteria in her voice.

"Lindsay," her father broke in, with firmness,"I've been talking about this with your mother. We would like you to do this, to at least make an attempt at getting involved. With Kathi helping you out, and Chris for company too, it'll never be easier."

"And if the show is over and done with and you didn't enjoy it at all, then we won't push you any more," her mother added smoothly.

Lindsay stared down at her plate miserably. She could feel the steel behind her parents' voices, and she knew she wasn't going to get out of it this time.

"So you're saying I have no choice," she said, in a low voice.

"If you want to put it that way, yes."

Lindsay sighed, and Kathi squeezed her hand. "It'll be fun, Lin, I promise. And then we can go to rehearsals together and with Chris too, if you want. It's fantastic to be a part of a show. You'll see."

"I guess I will," Lindsay said, with resignation, and then her mother changed the subject. Lin spent the rest of the meal trying to swallow something past the cold lump of dread lodged in her chest.

Lindsay and Chris pushed open the heavy auditorium doors after school the next day and scanned the dimly lit rows for Kathi. She waved them over from the stage apron, where she was perched with Mrs. Cummings.

"Lindsay," she said, as her sister came closer, "This is Mrs. Cummings, the director. Mrs. Cummings, my sister Lindsay."

"How are you, Lindsay," the director said warmly, extending a smooth hand to shake. Lindsay muttered something and barely remembered to introduce Chris. Kathi then led them over to their seats, and Mrs. Cummings gave her little speech to everyone.

"Thank you all for coming today," she said, to the rows of dim faces, "We're hoping for a really excellent show this year, and with the help of all of you it could be our best show yet. Camelot is a musical about King Arthur and his Knights of the Round Table. It is a romantic show, but also tragic in that Arthur is betrayed by his queen, Guinever, when she falls in love with one of Arthur's knights, Sir Lancelot."

"Now, for this production," Mrs. Cummings continued, shuffling through a sheaf of notes in her hand, "I'm looking for a large number of people for the chorus, to sing and dance as knights and ladies of the court. The leading roles you are probably already aware of, as they have been posted individually on the bulletin board."

"How will she find out whether we can sing or not?" Chris asked Kathi, leaning across Lindsay in the process.

"Oh, the music teacher will teach everyone a few lines of a song," Kathi replied airily, "Then you take turns singing it back."

"In private, I hope," Lindsay said, but Kathi shook her head.

"No, right here on the stage. Takes too long the other way, and besides, she has to know if you could sing in the show by yourself."

Lindsay's previous nervous tremors were nothing compared to the ones that assaulted her now. "You didn't warn me about this!" she hissed at Kathi, "Bad enough that I thought I'd just have to read lines alone, and now you tell me I have to sing...in public...all alone!"

"Don't be a jerk, Lin," Kathi said, with an unusual edge to her voice, "We've all had to do it. Don't be a wimp."

Lindsay considered bolting for the door, but Chris was blocking the way to the aisle. Instead she scrunched way down in her seat, hoping to be overlooked.

Kathi was among the first group called to audition. She read a small scene from the script, then effortlessly sang a section of one of Guinever's songs. Everyone clapped when she was done.

Chris was in the next group. She had been quiet while they were waiting, which was unusual for her, but once she got up on the stage Lindsay watched her light up as if a switch had been turned on.

She's pretending that she's Kathi, Lindsay said to herself suddenly, knowing how much her friend admired her older sister. And Chris did great: she read well, and she sang tunefully, although without Kathi's polish. Mrs. Cummings looked at her with interest, and made a note on Chris' audition sheet.

Lindsay's wish to be overlooked was futile, of course, and her name was called for the next group. She was shaking so badly that she had to clamp her teeth together to keep them from chattering. As always, when she was stressed, little bits of other people's emotions and thoughts came darting at her, but other people's nervousness didn't comfort her much.

The reading wasn't so bad, even if her voice was a little soft, and Lindsay actually felt slightly hopeful about the whole business. She listened intently as the music was taught—she played the piano, after all, so music came easily to her—then steeled herself for her turn.

"Lindsay? You're next." the music teacher prodded, and she took a deep quavering breath and opened her mouth.

Nothing. Nothing came out, just a breathy little squeak. Someone in the auditorium tittered, and Lindsay felt her face turn scarlet. She looked at Kathi for encouragement, and tried again. A little better this time…actual notes, but soft and wavering and barely in tune.

"Thank you, Lindsay," Mrs. Cummings interrupted smoothly, "Next?" Lindsay, dismissed, slunk back to her seat in humiliation. Chris gave her a sympathetic, if slightly superior, look, and Kathi patted her shoulder comfortingly.

"It wasn't so bad, now was it?" she whispered.

"It was worse." Lindsay replied flatly. Kathi studied her thoughtfully for a moment, but said nothing.

When the auditions were finished for the day, Kathi spent a few moments in discussion with Mrs. Cummings. Lindsay refused to think about what they were saying and whistled loudly and maddeningly to herself instead. Kathi came back without a word and they gathered up their things and headed for the late bus.

Chris pounced on Kathi as soon as they were outside.

"How did I do?" she asked, in a rush, "Do you think she liked me? Do you think I'll get a part?"

"You were good," Kathi replied patiently, "But you'll just have to wait and see, like everyone else."

"Well, at least I won't have to worry about the suspense," Lindsay grumbled, "There won't be any questions about my part."

"You should be happy," Kathi said coolly, "This way you won't have to worry about being involved in the play after all."

"Do you think I screwed up my audition on purpose?" Lindsay cried, hot tears springing to her eyes.

"Well, did you?"

"Oh, hell, yes, I just love to make an ass out of myself in front of half the school," Lindsay said, crying for real now. "I tried, Kath, I really did. After the reading I even thought I might have a chance."

"Oh, Lin," Kathi sighed, and gave her a little hug, "I'm sorry. I guess you were trying. I told Mrs. Cummings afterward that I knew you could sing fine in a group…I didn't say that I wasn't sure if you even wanted a chance."

"Well, I do," Lindsay snuffled, wiping her nose on her coat, "Don't ask me why…it'll only make Mom even more insufferable."

Kathi laughed, and passed her a Kleenex. Chris, who had been momentarily sidetracked by the appearance of Sam-from-English-class, rejoined them.

"Will Mrs. Cummings post the cast list tomorrow?" she demanded of Kathi.

"We'll see," Kathi replied, firmly, then, "C'mon, Lin, here's our bus. See you, Chris."

CHAPTER 4

Lindsay had to admit that her parents could be very patient with her. It made her feel guilty and defensive to know that she was the problem child of the family and the reason for a lot of head shaking on their part. Well, in all fairness, most of the shaking was her mom's, as her dad was not a terribly social person either, especially for a car salesman. But during the rest of the evening after the auditions, and the next morning, they never asked her a thing about it and looked the other way every time Lindsay's bad temper got the better of her.

When the bus came the next morning, Lindsay was actually relieved. She would go to the Drama Club bulletin board, her name would not be on the cast list, and life would go on as before. She wandered into school as casually as she could, spending a long time at her locker, combing her hair, putting away her books. She had just worked up the necessary frame of mind to approach the bulletin board when Chris came shrieking down the hall and grabbed her in a hug that felt like a head-on collision.

"I GOT A PART!" she screamed, for the benefit of everyone on the second floor.

Lindsay tried to look pleased as she disentangled herself and gathered up her strewn books.

"That's great, Chris!" she said with effort, but no real surprise. "What is it?"

"A real part, not just a chorus role," Chris informed her breathlessly, "A speaking role…Lady something-or-other…"

"A memorable role," Lindsay said sarcastically, but under her breath. Chris was so pretty and excited, standing there, and Lin felt drab and hopeless beside her.

"Well, I'm really glad for you," she said again, hoping it didn't sound as forced to Chris as it did to her ears.

"Hey, we should go see what part you got!" Chris exclaimed, finally remembering that Lin had also auditioned. She dragged her off down the hall. There was a big crowd of kids there, glued to the cast list, and a mixture of ecstatic and crestfallen faces. Lindsay felt a flutter of panic, and she let Chris push her way through and scan the list again.

Finally Chris turned and gave her an overly big smile. "Congrats, Lin, she's made you the props mistress!"

"What?" Lindsay squawked, and had to look for herself. Sure enough, there was her name, among the tech crew list. Props! Certainly not a job anyone would actually want! No part at all would be better than that…it smacked of pity.

Chris was trying to look sympathetic but wasn't succeeding very well, and Lindsay almost hated her. She had a sudden vision of the future where Chris reigned, beautiful and popular, and she was left in the dust. Lindsay used to be the one to shine: she read a little faster, came up with better ideas, got slightly better grades. But now Chris was in the lead, and definitely enjoying it. Later Lindsay could look back on that moment as the one when their friendship began to dissolve. It wasn't a dramatic thing, nothing was actually said and there was no argument, but it made a difference and they both knew it. It was an awkward moment until the bell suddenly rang and Mrs. Cummings appeared from within her office.

"Oh, hello Lindsay, and Christine," she said cheerfully, "Did you find your names on the cast lists?"

"Mrs. Cummings, I don't think I want to be…"

"I'd like to see you in my office for a moment," Mrs. Cummings interrupted, smoothly, "Will you excuse us, Christine?" Chris murmured something and started down the hall, looking back over her shoulder with frank curiosity.

The office was really just a cubbyhole, stuffed to the brim with books, papers, theatre posters, dirty coffee cups, and everything else. Mrs. Cummings unearthed a chair for Lindsay and then seated herself behind her desk, gazing at Lin searchingly until she squirmed with embarrassment and looked away.

Mrs. Cummings waited until Lindsay met her gaze again. She was an imposing woman and most everyone in school was afraid of her, even though Kathi insisted that she was wonderful.

After a moment she said, "I believe you were about to tell me that you didn't want to be props person."

"If it's all the same to you, I'd rather not be in the play at all," Lindsay replied quietly.

"It's not all the same to me," the director replied, sternly, "You auditioned, and while you did read well, your singing just isn't ready for a chorus role, even though you are lucky enough to have a sister who will vouch for your talent."

Lindsay's face burned.

"I know how badly Kathi wants you to be in this show," Mrs. Cummings continued, softening a little, "And I think you want it too, despite what you're telling me. However, it would look bad if I were to give you a part over someone who auditioned better than you did, simply because of Kathi's recommendation. Right?"

Lindsay nodded. It would look suspicious, especially to all the people who saw her terrible audition.

"So," Mrs. Cummings said, briskly, "Let's put you on stage crew. Working behind the scenes is a good introduction to the theatre, and perhaps next time you'll be more at ease and give us a better idea of what you can do. Kathi also tells me you were largely coerced into trying out anyway, so I'm not surprised that it didn't go well."

"Is there anything Kathi didn't tell you?" Lindsay remarked dryly, having found her voice again, and Mrs. Cummings laughed richly.

"Not much," she replied. "Will you do the job for us, Lindsay? It requires good organization and creativity, and I'll need to be able to count on you."

Lindsay thought for a moment. Organization and creativity. Well, she was pretty good in those departments, and she wouldn't have to perform in front of anyone.

"All right," she said, finally, "I'll do it."

Mrs. Cummings' grin transformed her face into something more closely approximating the kind of person Kathi insisted she was. She held out her hand and Lindsay shook it awkwardly.

"We'll have our first full meeting of cast and crew tomorrow afternoon," she said, "I'll give you the props list then." She then scrawled a late pass for Lindsay to take to homeroom, and gave it to her dismissively.

Lindsay emerged from her office feeling slightly dazed, but actually pretty good. There was some sort of warmth in Mrs. Cummings that made Lin like her, and the whole day was a bit brighter after their conversation.

CHAPTER 5

Lindsay found it had been much easier to tell Mrs. Cummings that she'd be props person than to actually do the job. Because "Camelot" took place in medieval times, the props she needed weren't exactly lying around in people's attics. Lindsay had to overcome her irrational fear of calling people on the telephone and actually contact other theatre groups to lend things, as well as scouring thrift shops and flea markets. But she had to admit, after a while, that it was sort of fun, like a big scavenger hunt.

On a Tuesday afternoon, about three weeks after auditions, Lindsay came running into the kitchen from late bus. Mom had quickly become accustomed to having Lin and Kathi bounce in a few minutes before supper, often bouncing out again an hour or so later. But she was pleased that the "get Lindsay involved" scheme had worked so well.

"Lindsay?" she yelled, from the pantry, "There's a package for you on the mail table!"

Lindsay thumped back down the stairs after depositing her books in her room. She didn't often receive much in the way of mail. The package was in the front hall, and she knew instantly that it was from Aunt Sam, by all the brightly-colored stamps with pictures of the Queen on them. Lin picked it up, hefting it curiously in her hands. Hmm. It felt like a book...

She wandered back into the kitchen where Mom was putting supper on the table, peeling the wrapping off as she walked. Finally the last shreds came away and it was a book, very old in appearance with a faded maroon cover and gilt lettering on the spine, almost illegible with age.

"Whatcha got?" Kathi inquired, coming in and taking off her coat. As usual, she had taken twice as long coming home from the bus stop because of all the blathering she did with her friends.

"It's a book from Aunt Sam," Lindsay replied, slowly piecing together the old printing. "It's called <u>Le</u> <u>Morte</u> <u>de</u> <u>Arthur</u>. What does that mean?"

"Something about death," Kathi said helpfully, from her vast knowledge of two years of Latin. "Arthur's death, I guess."

Mom wiped off her hands and came over. "Oh," she said, looking at the book, "Yes, it's French…The Death of Arthur. It's a classic by a man named Malory, and it tells all of the legends of King Arthur. I told Samantha you were working on the show, and she must have sent you this so that you could read the legends for yourself."

"Geez, she didn't send me anything," Kathi said petulantly, looking through the shredded wrappings.

"That's because she knows you won't read a book unless someone forces you," Lindsay told her sarcastically.

"That's true," Kathi replied, with good-natured honestly. She fingered the book. "It looks old. I wonder why she didn't send you a new copy?"

'I like it," Lindsay replied simply, turning the book over in her hands and feeling how well-worn the binding was from the use of many hands. She turned to the flyleaf:

Dear Lindsay (it said),

This was my favorite book when I was your age. I hope you'll love it as much as I did. It should make Camelot come alive for you.

All my love,
Samantha

Lindsay read the inscription several times before surrendering the book for family scrutiny. It made her feel like an adult, to see that her aunt had signed herself with her first name alone. Kathi handed the book back and Lin looked closely at the marbled endpapers, where she could faintly see the name "Samantha Ellerton" in round childish handwriting, the pencilled letters now almost invisible. She turned a few pages, but Mom was herding everyone to supper so she decided not to start reading. It was a special book and it deserved her undivided attention.

Things going as they usually do, Lindsay didn't have a chance to look at the book again that evening, so on impulse she stuck it into her book bag the next morning as she was running to catch the bus. There was a marathon rehearsal and tech session scheduled after school and continuing into the evening, so she knew she'd have a break at some point to begin reading about King Arthur and his court.

After school, Lindsay made her way to the auditorium. Mrs. Cummings was beginning to rehearse the jousting scene on the bare stage, and Lin could hear Chris' shrill laugh even from the props closet backstage.

"Sounds as if at least Chris is getting into the spirit of things," Alice remarked, coming up behind Lindsay with several cans of paint. "We're about to paint the castle backdrop…can you help?"

"Okay," Lindsay replied, stashing her book bag in the closet, "Mrs. Cummings isn't ready to use props yet, so I might as well be doing something." She followed Alice across the rear of the stage and out the big double doors to the work area.

"Hi, Lindsay!" someone called, from a big group of "techies" who were assembling the big castle wall sections.

"Hi," Lindsay answered, a bit shyly.

"I convinced her to help us out," Alice said, putting down the paint cans and rubbing her sore arms, "The props business not being too brisk at the moment."

"It sounds like a herd of elephants stampeding out there, instead of a joust," one of the guys—Jeff, Lindsay thought his name was—said, "And someone's whinneying like a pony."

"That would be Chris," Lindsay said evenly, and to her surprise they all laughed.

"Ah, yes, the new Miss Drama Club insider," Alice said wickedly, "To listen to her, you'd think she was a senior who'd been in every show."

There were more laughs, and Lindsay tried not to feel disloyal. Chris was asking for it, though: these days she went around mimicking drama club banter and inside jokes in a particularly infuriating way. There was a big difference between the Drama Club actors and the techies, and Chris knew it. Lindsay wasn't in her league anymore. Lindsay, for her part, preferred the backstage people. They were nice and honest and she actually felt comfortable with them, more than any other group she'd ever encountered in high school.

Alice slapped a paintbrush into her hand and she sat down on the floor, carefully painting in the outlines of stones that Jeff was pencilling on the wooden walls.

"Lindsay, you're Kathi's sister, aren't you?" Jeff asked, after a moment.

"Yes," Lindsay replied warily, "Why?"

"Oh, I don't know," Jeff said, calmly, "You just don't seem very much like her, that's all. Are you just biding time here with the techies,'til the day comes for your big stage debut?"

Lindsay thought that one over for a moment. "I don't know," she answered truthfully, "A few weeks ago I wanted a part, but now I think I'd rather be back here."

Jeff smiled at her, so she knew she'd given the right answer. He was quite cute when he smiled.

Before she knew it, it was time for supper and Mrs. Cummings called for a break. Most kids took off downtown for pizza or burgers.

"We're going out for fast food," Alice said to Lindsay, as they were washing their hands, "Want to come?"

Lindsay shook her head, a little regretfully. 'I brought my stuff with me," she explained.

"Okay…but next time, plan on it!" Alice said, and Lin nodded, pleased. Alice left with Jeff and a few others, and Lin almost changed her mind about going. But she hadn't had much peace lately, and wanted to relax and read Aunt Sam's book.

Soon the auditorium was empty and quiet. Lindsay looked at the scarred backstage walls with dissatisfaction and decided to take her sandwich and soda out on the stage, where it was bright and much warmer. She found a comfortable spot, legs dangling over the edge of the stage apron and her back resting against the piano.

With her sandwich in one hand, Lin opened the book. The worn cover and thick ivory pages had a silky feel. She turned to the beginning of the story:

"King Uther Pendragon, ruler of all Britain, had been at war for many years with the Duke of Tintagel in Cornwall when he was told of the beauty of Lady Igraine, the duke's wife…"

Lindsay felt rather peculiar. The dense, old-fashioned printing wavered in front of her eyes, and she wondered if someone was fooling with the stage lighting. She rubbed her eyes furiously, but the letters continued to swim on the page. She was beginning to feel heavy-eyed and pleasantly drowsy. Maybe it was too warm here, under all the lights…She put her food down and rested her eyes for a moment, still seeing the printed words against the inside of her eyelids. It was such a welcoming sensation, the grayness just before sleep, and Lindsay couldn't fight it. The book slid off her lap and came to rest, still opened, on the stage floor, her hand on the page. Her head nodded and she was oblivious.

CHAPTER 6

"I can't believe that we've finally left that convent for good! No more beastly Latin, or reading ancient crumbling books, or chess…"

"I don't know. It was rather peaceful. We didn't have to worry about finding husbands, or being invaded, or running a household."

"Husbands!" a third voice exclaimed. "I can't wait to return home, and have my father find me a husband. Now that we are properly educated, our betrothals will take place right away. And you will have your wedding, Alyce."

Lindsay drifted back into consciousness against the chatter of these unfamiliar voices. Had rehearsal begun again, while she napped here in full view on the stage? How embarrassing. She could only hope that she wasn't snoring, as Kathi told her she often did. Lindsay struggled to wake up.

Something was odd. There was a gentle jogging motion beneath her…perhaps just the thud of heavy feet on the stage floor? Sunlight played across her face, and the air had an underlying fresh smell, a greenness that didn't belong in a stuffy auditorium. The continued motion was oddly familiar, bringing back memories of summer camp and riding old swaybacked horses.

Lindsay opened her eyes finally, cautiously, wondering if she were the butt of one of those famed exotic Drama Club practical jokes. As soon as she blinked, however, she knew that something was drastically wrong. No joke she'd ever heard of could possibly be this elaborate, unless it involved a Hollywood movie studio.

Lindsay found herself seated on a slowly moving horse, dappled gray, placidly plodding along with its nose close to the rough path ahead of it, occasionally swatting her with its tail as it slapped at flies. She was traveling through an immense forest, with trees that were tremendous in size and looked infinitely older than anything she'd ever seen in New Hampshire before. And even more starting to her sleep-blurred senses were the people surrounding her, also on horseback, whose bright voices filled the air like a flock of companionable birds chattering in the morning sun.

"How much longer?" someone whined, ahead.

"Hours and hours," someone else replied, nastily, "For heaven's sake, Mary, complaining won't make the time pass faster."

This conversation, as well as the one Lindsay had first overheard, was coming from a group of three girls who looked to be roughly her same age. Lindsay studied them intently.

Their faces were like the faces of young women anywhere, reflecting cheerful personalities or unhappy ones, but their clothing sent a shiver of fear and unreality down her spine. She had never seen clothing like this, except in a costume book: long, brightly colored tunics and gowns, topped by shorter tunics or cloaks, and with elaborate cloth headdresses covering their long braids of hair. They were a pretty contrast with the greens and browns of the forest, in their reds and purples and yellows. The garments looked well made, of rich fabrics, and the girls wore bright jewelry.

Lindsay took a deep breath before looking down at herself, and again she felt that nudge of fear. She, too, wore a similar costume: a long blue gown covered by a short purple tunic and a lavender cape clasped with a jeweled brooch. Her hair was gathered into a rather untidy braid, and on her feet she wore low leather boots. She studied these with more interest, holding her foot out from the horse's side and turning it a little.

They looked just like what many of the girls in school were wearing, and she giggled, but all in all her outfit was a far cry from the jeans and sweatshirt she'd started out in that morning.

Lindsay's giggle had attracted attention. An older woman, riding in a group ahead of the girls, turned to look back and then effortlessly reined her horse up beside Lindsay's. She was perhaps a bit older than Lin's mom, with graying hair and a well-worn face, but she too was elegantly dressed.

"I'm glad to see that you've awakened, Lindsay," she said, in a warm voice, and smiled. "Not too many more miles, and then you will be reunited with your family again." She reached out and smoothed back some of the stray wisps of hair that were plastered against Lindsay's cheeks, a gesture that showed both familiarity and affection.

Lindsay felt a flash of hope when the woman spoke of her family. Was it all a prank after all, and around the corner they'd find Kathi and her friends, all giggling madly at the success of their joke? The woman had called her Lindsay, so her name was still her own. Was it an odd dream, brought on by too much "Camelot"? Lindsay opened her mouth to ask a question, then suddenly closed it again. Some primitive sense of self-preservation warned her not to expose herself until she knew what was going on.

So Lindsay just smiled at the woman, and then began looking around again. Other than the three girls and some older women, most of the little caravan on horseback seemed to consist of armed men with crossbows and swords, and not a gun in sight. Lindsay tried craning her neck to see ahead over the vista of horse's ears and women's heads, but all she could really discover was that the men rode easily, calling out amiable insults to each other. They seemed to ignore the women, whom she decided they were supposed to be guarding.

There was no other explanation. It must be a very realistic dream, brought on by too many dusty old library books about the middle ages, which Lin had been reading for inspiration on props. She'd simply been living and breathing "Camelot" for too many weeks now. Lindsay liked this explanation, even though she knew that it wasn't going to keep her satisfied for very long if she didn't wake up soon. She couldn't remember a dream being quite this vivid before.

The girls ahead of Lindsay began conversing again, this time speaking with the older women. They were expending a great deal of energy discussing people and events that Lin knew nothing about: births, deaths, marriages, and housekeeping, among other topics. It sounded like Lin's mom and grandmother at every family reunion she could remember. However, they seemed to be questioning each other rhetorically, not expecting any answers, the way people do when they've been away from a place for a long time and are anxious and excited about going back and seeing what is happening. They needed to talk about familiar things but weren't expecting any answers. Lindsay got so interested in listening that she urged her horse a little further ahead, until it walked right up on the heels of one of the girls' mares. She gave a breathy little shriek as her horse skittered sideways, clinging to the saddle most ungracefully and sending Lindsay a nasty look.

"For being such an expert horsewoman, you're certainly having trouble controlling that old plow horse," she said scathingly. Lindsay returned her look guilelessly. If that was an insult, it was pretty much wasted on her. However, the girl continued to glare, so Lindsay let her horse fall back a little ways. Everyone seemed to know who she was, but she didn't have a clue as to who they were and what the situation was. She was definitely at a disadvantage.

Lindsay now noticed that all three girls wore clothing that was somewhat more elegant than her own, especially that of the girl named Alyce, who was very pretty, blonde and blue-eyed with flawless skin. The other two seemed to look up to her deferentially. Lindsay looked down at her own clothing again, noticing this time that there were stains on her tunic and a tear in her gown's hem. She sighed. Even in a dream, it seemed that she was once again on the outside of the group and not wearing the right clothes. Some things never changed.

The girl whose horse had started continued her glare for a few more calculated moments, then flounced straight in her saddle again, making very audible comments about people who aspired beyond their positions, but no amount of education could ever disguise a peasant. It was meant to be insulting but was just confusing: Lindsay hadn't the slightest idea what she was talking about. Finally the same older woman who had spoken to Lindsay said something to this girl as well, and she fell silent. Then the woman spoke to Lin again.

"Pay her no mind, Lindsay," she said quietly, "An idle tongue is the Devil's tool. Lady Mary is still flaunting her title like a new dress, and begrudging you your education because it was a gift from the lord to your father."

The dream excuse was definitely wearing thin. Her father? Lindsay could only imagine what her dad would say if she wanted to be educated at a convent! And if this were really a dream, shouldn't these girls all have familiar faces, maybe those of Chris and the sophomore popularity queens she was beginning to hang around with?

Lindsay just shrugged with what she hoped was a resigned-but-brave expression, not daring to speak. The woman smiled, and then gave her a tweak on the arm.

"Now, then," she said, suddenly businesslike, "See what you can do about neatening your hair and brushing out your skirts, before we are in sight of the castle. Your father won't let us within the gates if you arrive as you are!" With that, she bustled ahead, stopping to make a few comments to the other women.

Castle? Oh, this was definitely getting worse. Lindsay's chest tightened with fear again.

"Please, oh please let me wake up now," she whispered to herself, pinching herself on the arm for good measure. She dusted off the alien long skirts, as best as she could, but there wasn't much help for her hair, without a comb or mirror. She settled for running her fingers through the most tangled wisps, to the amusement of Lady Mary and her friends.

Suddenly there was a glad exclamation from the women ahead, and the rough road that they had been following gradually broke free from the trees and into the bright sunshine of open space and cultivated fields. Lindsay noticed farmers working beside the road and a large woman walking along with a load of straw on her back, but then she gazed further along the fields and became open-mouthed with shock.

At the end of the road, situated above the surrounding countryside on a slight hill, stood a real castle, looming gray and massive and bustling with activity.

CHAPTER 7

Lindsay was only familiar with two types of castles. One was the big blue and white Disneyland castle, complete with perpetual fireworks and Tinkerbell flitting around. The others were those huge, depressing ruins in her history book, crumbling walls that didn't look like anyone could ever have called them home. Well, with those in mind, it was even more of a shock to really see the castle that they were now approaching at a quickening pace.

It was a good-sized building, to her eyes, with high walls of well-fitted gray stones and two towers rising from opposite corners. Cheerful banners stirred and floated in the breeze, making it look festive. As their little procession began climbing the rise to the castle, they curved slightly to the left until she could see that the castle actually enveloped a whole town, spread out in the protective shadow of its walls. Streets of small houses radiated out from a huge gateway, and the main street of the village made a straight line to the fields below. And everywhere it was bustling with the traffic of people and animals.

Lindsay thought of dull old Mr. Stevens, her history teacher, and his stuffy, droning lectures on ancient history. According to him, life in a castle was a drab, dull affair, spiced up only by the occasional siege or war, with a few knights coming and going. But gazing open-mouthed before her now, Lindsay couldn't believe how incredibly alive this place was: the streets were noisy with throngs of people in all types of clothing, cows and pigs and chickens running free, and bright garden patches amongst the churned muddy streets. How could this scene ever become one of Mr. Stevens' boring classes, where everyone passed notes and didn't even bother to cover up their yawns?

Suddenly Lindsay choked and gagged. As her horse swung onto the main street, they rode into a cloud of the most disgusting smell she'd ever smelled. It was even worse than the time they'd had the septic tank pumped. Later on she would discover that it was exactly the same thing: raw sewage. Apparently they hadn't heard too much about sanitation. Something else Mr. Stevens had never bothered to mention.

She was so busy trying to hold her breath against the stench, while at the same time avoiding the mud that threatened to spatter her clothes as the horse's hooves flipped it up, that she didn't notice the crowd gathering around them until her horse stopped short.

"Lindsay, daughter!" A short, stocky man with an air of authority and a pleasant, round face practically pulled her off the horse and hugged her. "How good it is to see you, girl! How was the journey? Have you learned much at the convent these two years? How you have changed! Ready to settle down now, I'll wager."

Alarmed, Lindsay just stood there letting him embrace her, totally at a loss. Settle down…what did that mean? Was this man her father? How could that be?

A voice spoke calmly from behind her. It was the older woman who had spoken to her in the forest, and she smoothed Lindsay's hair while speaking past her to the man.

"You should be proud of your daughter, Sir Thomas," she said, smiling, "Two years at her studies, and glowing reports from the sisters. And much improved in appearance and deportment, although it may not be apparent at the moment."

Lindsay silently blessed her for providing at least a name for this man.

"Of course I am proud, Mistress Dorothy," Sir Thomas replied, also smiling, "As her mother will be also, when she sees her."

Mother? Probably another stranger. Lindsay closed her eyes briefly and prayed that she might wake up NOW.

"Where is mother?" Lindsay said breathily, just for the sake of saying something. A look passed between Mistress Dorothy and Sir Thomas.

"Now, Lindsay," Dorothy said, in a gentle rebuke, "You know that your lady mother is unwell and must confine herself to her chamber. Perhaps we shall call upon her tomorrow, when you have rested."

Lindsay nodded. A small boy relieved her of her horse, and she was rather sorry to see him go. He was the most familiar thing she had right now. A wave of overwhelming homesickness washed over her and stung her eyes with sudden tears. Where was she? Where was Kathi, and school, and home, and her parents? What was she doing here, with these people who seemed to know her, and strangers who called themselves her family? The comfort of thinking it was all a dream was slipping away fast.

Mistress Dorothy took her arm and piloted her across the slippery stones of the street, through the massive gateway, and into the castle's courtyard. She kept a respectful distance behind Sir Thomas, who obviously held some sort of high rank in this place, but the system of who rated higher than who was beyond Lindsay. One of those feudalism things she'd probably glossed over in her history book.

They approached a large door made of wood and reinforced by metal bands. As Lindsay was ushered inside, she stumbled and blinked several times in the sudden gloom. As soon as her eyes had adjusted from the bright sunshine outside, she found that they stood in a huge, open room. It had a rough wooden floor, mostly covered with straw or hay, and none too clean. She tried not to look to closely. Candles and oil lamps fastened to the walls shed a little light, and a huge fireplace dominated one wall, its fire just glowing embers at the moment. There were many long wooden tables, and at one end of the room was a raised platform with another single table. Who was the lucky person who got to sit there, to be stared at by everyone else?

Sir Thomas continued down the length of the room to a small screened hallway. He paused at the foot of a spiral staircase, made of stone. Here he gave Lindsay a fatherly kiss, and patted her hand.

"I'll leave you to go to your room now, daughter," he said, "We'll have an opportunity to talk after this evening's meal, and perhaps tomorrow we shall visit your mother." He returned to the large room, and Dorothy gently guided Lindsay up the stairs. She stumbled a little.

"Poor child," Dorothy said, soothingly, "A long day it's been, and a long journey. A good rest is what you need." She gave Lindsay a prompting push as she hesitated wearily on the steep stairs, and they continued climbing until they reached the next floor.

It must have been a bedroom, but it looked bare and cheerless. Lindsay noticed a few pieces of baggage that had been strapped to a packhorse, and her heart sank as she realized that this was her room. If it was possible to be more depressed than she had been a moment ago, then she was. She sank down on the large, curtained bed, which took up most of the room. It was very cold, even with sunlight streaming in through the small open window. No carpets, no pictures, just two wooden chests and a chair, and a rough mattress in one corner. A dark tapestry hung on one wall.

"Isn't it wonderful to be home again?" Dorothy exclaimed, as she bustled around unpacking garments and putting them away in the chests. "Back with family, although I'm sure you might miss those who you came to know so well at the convent. But your father is so proud of you, a convent-educated daughter when he is only a castle's seneschal, and just recently knighted. He should be able to find you a fine husband now, my sweet."

Husband? She had to be kidding, Lindsay thought dully. Who gets married at fifteen? She'd never even had a date, for heaven's sake. And just what was a seneschal, anyway?

"Yes, a good husband for you, and high time, young Lindsay," Dorothy continued, folding several dresses that seemed to be made of as much cloth as a small tent, "Why, when I was your age I was three years married with a little daughter of my own."

Lindsay couldn't help herself. "Married?" she squeaked, "How on earth can I possibly get married? I'm too young!" There, she'd finally said something. If this wasn't a dream, then who knew how long she could be stuck in someone else's life! She was going to look out for her own interests, and she certainly wasn't getting married.

Dorothy gave a sharp sigh, put down her armload of clothing, and sat down beside Lindsay. Taking her hand, she said, "We will not start this again, my girl. Be thankful that you were allowed two years of schooling at an age when you should have been betrothed. Your father has a soft heart where you are concerned, but he has his limits, too." She smoothed Lindsay's hair again. It seemed to be a characteristic gesture. "Make the best of it. You're home again with your family, and your father is in a better position than ever before to make a good match for you. And remember, even though your sister is married, she is here with us."

Lindsay wished she knew whether Dorothy was supposed to be her servant or her companion, because she already valued the woman's good opinion and hated to see her so anxious. It could be that Dorothy was going to be her only ally in this place. It wouldn't hurt to stay in her good graces.

"All right," Lindsay said, finally, "I won't talk about it again."-At least not until I know more about why I'm in this place, and for how long, she added silently.

Dorothy smiled at her once more, then straightened the bed covers, and helped her settle more comfortably on the bed. As soon as Lindsay closed her eyes, the confusing events of the day blurred a little and grew fainter. She wondered fleetingly if she would wake up in her own bed at home. It was a comforting thought, and she was asleep before Dorothy had even descended the stairs.

CHAPTER 8

Lindsay was amazed to find out what a creature of habit she was. As she drifted into wakefulness the next morning, she lay drowsing with her eyes closed, waiting for her mom to call her as she waited until the last possible moment to get up. Where was that first whiff of the incredibly strong coffee that her parents drank? And did she have an Algebra test today, or was that tomorrow?

Somewhere a sheep baaed, then several more, and Lindsay frowned a little at the unfamiliar noises. There was a low buzz of many voices, which she just couldn't place, until she finally opened her eyes. Gray stone walls. Curtains around her bed. A sliver of sunshine coming in the window.

Lindsay groaned, and sat up slowly, feeling disoriented. If the whole castle thing was a dream, then why was she still here? The idea that this could be a hoax of some kind, and she the innocent victim, unfortunately didn't seem to work as an explanation anymore, and she let it go reluctantly. Slowly she swung her feet out from under the heavy coverlet and put them down gingerly on the ice-cold floor. She tossed her tangled hair out of her eyes and sighed. Some things hadn't changed: it was still hard to get out of bed.

Yawning, she glanced around self-consciously. Was she supposed to get dressed and go down into the big hall, where all the voices seemed to be coming from? Or was she supposed to wait for Dorothy to come fetch her, and lead her to where she should be? It was like being a guest in someone's house and not knowing the routine or the house rules.

Lindsay decided that she could at least be finding something to put on, and went over to one of the big wooden chests. She began to paw tentatively through the unfamiliar garments. Being someone mostly used to sweatshirts and jeans, with an occasional skirt, the voluminous and mostly unidentifiable pieces of cloth that she kept pulling out were a complete mystery. She couldn't even tell what was supposed to be worn where. What if she got dressed and went downstairs in some totally wrong combination of clothes? It could be extremely embarrassing. Fortunately, Dorothy seemed to have some kind of motherly telepathy, and she bustled in before Lindsay was completely buried in fabric.

"Lindsay," she said, clucking her tongue in disapproval, "I just finished putting all those things away! I've already set out clothing for you on the other chest."

"Oh," Lindsay replied, blushing guiltily and picking up the gown and tunic. Dorothy seemed to expect her to dress right then and there, so she slowly stripped off her nightdress and was astounded to find that she was not wearing one stitch of underwear.

As fast as possible, Lindsay put the nightdress back on.

"Oh, I put a clean shift there, too," Dorothy said, from where she was refolding all the clothing. She passed Lindsay another long, thin gown, this one crinkled into pleats, and Lin quickly exchanged it for the nightgown. Then she put the other heavy, slightly musty garments on, feeling hopelessly clumsy and inept. Where, oh where was her comfortable twentieth century underwear?

"Mercy!" Dorothy suddenly yanked the tunic down over Lin's head. "Your father is waiting for you at breakfast, and here you are dawdling." She pummeled Lindsay into the tunic as ruthlessly as if she were a pillow to be stuffed into a pillowcase, then took a comb to her hair, yanking it out by the roots. Finally, she rummaged around in a small velvet box that had come out of the luggage, and took out a beautiful necklace with a glowing stone. She fastened it around Lindsay's neck with a satisfied smile.

"There. Your father will be proud to see you this morning. The necklace finally seems to suit you."

For the first time, Lindsay wondered about the other girl whose place she seemed to be taking, the other Lindsay who didn't want to get married and was too unkempt to wear an emerald necklace. If Lindsay was here now, was the other girl taking her place? It was a scary thought.

"Come along now," Dorothy said, commandingly, and ushered Lindsay down the stairs, none too gently. Lin felt her heart begin to flutter in her chest. Now she would have to come face to face with all the inhabitants of this place, all without giving away the fact that she was a complete and total stranger. The idea of announcing that she was some time visitor from the future never entered her mind: one thing Mr. Stevens had told them about in history class, with great relish, were the medieval methods for dealing with people who might appear to be witches.

Dorothy and Lindsay descended the stairs and came out into the great hall, and Lindsay felt her mouth drop open. She hadn't exactly been expecting stiff, gray little knights and expressionless women in pointed hats, but neither had she expected this big crowd of lively people, eating and talking and laughing, while a small army of serving people threaded their way between the tables, balancing plates of food. Dorothy led her to a table set apart at the side of the room, slightly below the high table, which was obviously for the resident lord. Or was it a king? Did every castle have a king and queen, or could lesser people live in them, too?

Dorothy's guiding hand eased her forward until she was face to face with her "father", Sir Thomas. She stood at awkward attention until he finished a conversation with a young man beside him, who looked exactly like him and must therefore be Lindsay's brother.

"Ah, daughter!" he said finally, looking at her with obvious approval, "How well you look! A world of difference from when you left us. Be seated, and have your breakfast."

Dorothy suddenly melted away, and Lindsay panicked a little at being left absolutely on her own. It took her a moment to decide exactly how to negotiate sitting on the bench without displaying her lack of underwear to the entire room, but finally she tucked her skirts under the table and sat down, her face only slightly pink.

Sir Thomas covered her hand with his own and gave it a squeeze before returning to his conversation. His eyes had the same mixture of friendliness and love that Lindsay's own dad had, and she felt better, sitting there with him, despite another sharp stab of homesickness.

A serving woman set food down in front of Lindsay. There was no plate, only a piece of bread that seemed to be used as a sort of edible plate. A wooden cup held some sort of bitter wine made Lin wrinkle her nose in distaste. From a platter set down next to her, she took some sort of cheese and a slice of cold meat. It wasn't that appetizing, but she was starved. Thinking longingly of orange juice, a raspberry Danish, maybe some Captain Crunch cereal, Lindsay took a nibble of the bread. It tasted funny, but she was too hungry to care.

Sir Thomas didn't seem to expect her to talk, so she took advantage of her position and gazed out over the rest of the hall. It was so hard to believe that these people were real, living and breathing, their clothes bright and new, and not the faded, dull things found in museum exhibits. If this was really a normal, typical day in a castle, then these people before her were just as alive and regular as the kids in Lindsay's first period Algebra class. But why, and how, was she here, marooned on her own, without even enough history classes to smooth out some of the rough spots? The United States and everything else she knew were an awful lot of years down the road. Her only consolation was knowing that her Aunt Sam would kill to be in her place right now.

Lindsay bravely swallowed the bread and cheese and gagged on the wine, took an experimental bite of the meat and abandoned it, and half listened to Sir Thomas' conversation. Scanning the crowd of people again, she suddenly realized that someone was staring at her from a far corner of the room. It was a young man, with a dark, rather sullen face, dark hair, and the most amazing intense eyes. Lindsay held his gaze only for a moment and then looked away, embarrassed, like she'd been caught looking at something forbidden. But even after she turned her face away and looked meekly at her food, she could still feel his eyes upon her.

Sir Thomas was finally rising from the bench, and Lindsay wondered wildly what she was supposed to do now. How did they expect her to spend her day? Thankfully, Dorothy materialized at her elbow.

"Come along, Lady Lindsay," she said, a bit grimly, "Your lady mother has requested your presence in her chamber." Still thinking of those intense eyes, but not daring to sneak another look at the young man, Lindsay docilely let Dorothy lead her away.

CHAPTER 9

Dorothy ushered Lindsay out of the hall and back up the stairs with a firm hand on her elbow. Lindsay had discovered that morning that her room was really just a glorified hallway, as several people had passed through while she was in bed. Dorothy proceeded through Lin's room and through several other empty sleeping chambers until they came to a doorway hung with a concealing curtain. Lindsay was impressed: this was as much privacy as she'd seen anyone have in this place. At least back home her own room had a lock on the door, even if her mom did get mad when she used it.

Dorothy drew the curtain aside almost timidly and gave Lindsay another gentle shove into the room. Lin was beginning to feel like some sort of puppet that people just placed where they wanted. It took her eyes several moments to adjust to the gloom, for despite the warm autumn day outside, the window was shuttered and the only light was from the large fire burning in the hearth. It was stifling hot and there was an unpleasant mustiness, as if there hadn't been any fresh air in years.

"Over to the bed, Lindsay," Dorothy hissed, and Lindsay sidled over before Dorothy could shove her again. Dorothy cleared her throat gently and was rewarded with a sharp voice, coming from the depths of the mattress.

"Who is it?" the voice demanded, in a petulant, nasally tone.

"Milady," Dorothy said quickly, pushing Lindsay forward, "I've brought your lady daughter to see you." Lindsay started as a finger painfully poked her back and Dorothy whispered that she should curtsey. It was definitely an acquired skill, Lindsay thought ruefully, as she gave an awkward little bob that nearly landed her on the floor. And just how many bruises was she going to have after a day of Dorothy's fingers?

"Lindsay?" The voice coming from the pillow was noticeably weaker, but it sounded to Lin like the person was trying to sound weak. "Come closer, daughter, and let me look upon you."

Lindsay moved still closer until she could clearly see this woman who was supposed to be her mother. She had a sharp face, but she was beautiful in a fuzzy, invalidish sort of way. She was wearing some kind of ornate cap and a shift with ornate embroidery around the neck. But she didn't look like an especially pleasant woman, and Lindsay was thankful that she wasn't really her mother.

"Ah, daughter," the woman said, as Lin came clearly into her range of vision, "Well, it seems that your education has had some good effect upon you, for your appearance has certainly improved. Turn around, child." Lindsay spun clumsily, stifling the urge to giggle. It was the same thing her grandmother always made her do.

After thoroughly inspecting her with her sharp gaze, the woman sank back onto her pillows with a sigh, putting on an expression of weariness again. "I'm glad to have you home again, child. Perhaps now we can accomplish something in teaching you household management and seeing you married well. Then my mind will be at ease, with both of my daughters settled." She gave a big pathetic sigh and gestured tiredly toward a dark corner by the hearth. "Greet your sister, Lindsay. Were you told that she was back with us, while her husband is away? And then leave me in peace, for I am unutterably weary."

Lindsay thought with irritation that the woman had missed her calling. She would be great on a soap opera. However, nothing more seemed to be expected of her, so she turned to where this sister was, ready to give a curtsey or two and then get out of there.

The woman stepped forward to meet Lindsay, but against the bright flames of the fire only her profile was visible: tall, slim, with hair bound away from her face and the kind of high cheekbones Lin had always coveted. Her long skirts rustled against the floor, and something about her walk was naggingly familiar, especially here where everyone was a stranger.

The woman came closer and reached out to embrace Lindsay, and as her face came into the light Lin gasped and felt the room begin to spin. She'd always been so scornful of those heroines in movies who fainted for the least reason, but suddenly she had some idea of what it was like. The woman hurriedly gathered her into her arms just as Lindsay's knees began to buckle, and Lin had only a moment to see the bemused and loving expression in Aunt Sam's eyes before she buried her face in her shoulder and shut her eyes tightly.

Lindsay clung to her aunt like a little kid, as a sudden source of security in this whole bewildering mess. "Is it really you, Aunt Sam?" she whispered.

"Hush," her aunt replied, hugging her reassuringly. She managed to maneuver Lindsay back beyond the curtained doorway.

"She'll be fine in a moment, Milady Samantha," Dorothy said anxiously, hovering nearby, "A bit wearying it is, to see her lady mother again after two years away, and then yourself as well. You two were always such great companions...She's just a bit overcome, is all." Lindsay was comforted by the affection in Dorothy's voice, even as she clung to her aunt.

"Thank you, Dorothy," Samantha said smoothly, her faintly British accent just the same as it had always been. Lindsay wondered irrelevantly if she herself still sounded All-American. Aunt Sam always made her self-conscious about how she spoke.

"I think my little sister and I will walk in the gardens," Aunt Sam was saying, drawing Lindsay out of her embrace and tucking the girl's hand inside the crook of her elbow.

"A good idea," Dorothy responded, with obvious relief, "I've much to attend to downstairs." She smoothed Lindsay's hair and tweaked her skirts, then disappeared back through the maze of rooms until they could hear her light step descending the stairs. Only then did Lindsay turn to confront her aunt.

"What in the world are you doing here?" Lindsay began, almost hysterically, "Or should I say, what am I doing here?" Lin went from insecure to angry all of a sudden. She wanted answers to all of the questions of the past two days, and she had a feeling that Aunt Sam would provide them.

"Shh...!" her aunt said, glancing at the curtained door, "Lady Rosamunde may appear sickly, but her hearing is especially acute. Don't let her fool you. We can talk in the gardens."

With that, she led Lindsay back downstairs and outside, threading her way expertly through passages and gateways until they were in the formal gardens. The sun shone down warmly on Lindsay's bare head. She took a deep breath of fresh air, and then turned to Aunt Sam.

CHAPTER 10

The garden was sheltered, enclosed by the walls of the castle. Aunt Sam gracefully lifted her long skirts and led the way along the graveled path to a secluded stone bench. The garden was tinged with the gold and bronze of autumn, summer's green remaining only in the grass and a few plants. The sun was still warm, however, as Lindsay sank down onto the bench, not so gracefully, owing to her unfamiliarity with long skirts. Aunt Sam seemed to be much better at it.

"There," she said, with a sigh, "This is much more private. Go ahead, Lindsay."

Lindsay sat there for a moment. There were about a million questions that she needed to ask and she had absolutely no idea where to begin. After chewing her lower lip ragged for a few moments, she finally came out with the question that had bothered her most since this whole experience began.

"All right," Lindsay began, hesitantly, "I guess what bothers me the most is that I just don't know what's going on here. First I thought it was all some big practical joke that the drama club crew was playing on me. Then I decided it had to all be a dream, except that I'm not having any luck at all trying to wake up. And now, seeing you here...I can't decided if you're just part of my dream, or if we're both crazy."

Her aunt looked overwhelmed for a moment, but then laughed softly. "Well, I can try to assure you that we're not crazy, but I suppose that if I was crazy I wouldn't know it anyway! And if it's a dream, then I've been dreaming for a long time now, and at my own will to choose my dream. And if it's a joke, then it's on both of us, for I certainly didn't expect you to come riding into the courtyard yesterday."

"So if it's not a dream, or a joke, or insanity, then what is it?"

Aunt Sam sighed, smoothing her skirts with a weary expression. "I wish I had an easy answer for you, Lin," she said, "But I don't have one for myself yet, and I've been here much longer."

"Well, maybe you should tell me how you got here, then," Lindsay said, a bit rudely.

"Well..." She seemed oddly reluctant, but then she smiled at Lindsay. "Perhaps. And by the way, you had better get used to calling me Samantha, as we are supposed to be sisters."

Lindsay was rather pleased with that idea. Aunt Sam would be a lot more fun to have around than Kathi or Andrea, that was for sure. She tucked her knees up under her chin in a most unladylike manner.

"It's taken me a while to work out for myself what happened," Samantha began, "As you know, it's such a shock trying to adjust to your surroundings here, to find that you're suddenly a part of everything and yet so alien. At least you'll have the advantage of having me here to help you out. I've only been coming here for a few months, and it was entirely accidental. I was poking around an antiquarian bookshop in London when I stumbled onto a book of medieval legends. It wasn't much of a book, more old than valuable, but it seemed interesting so I bought it. It was several weeks later before I got around to reading it, and when I opened the cover...well, I'm sure you know about the rest. As I began reading, things hazed over, and when I awoke I was here."

"How did you know that a book brought me here?" Lindsay asked her suspiciously. "I don't seem to remember telling you that."

Samantha turned to her with a grin. "Oh, come now, Lin, haven't you figured it out yet?" Lindsay continued to stare at her, mystified, until her aunt laughed and took Lin's chin in her hand.

"Don't you know, Lindsay, that telepathy tends to run in families?"

Lindsay felt her jaw drop. She stared at her aunt, open-mouthed, then blushed foolishly.

"So it was true!" she said, "The feeling I had, any time I tried to listen to your thoughts…as if you were laughing at me, and knew exactly what I was up to!"

"And so I did," her aunt replied smugly, "I've been waiting to see if you would ever get around to confronting me about it."

Lindsay glowered at her. "Not likely. About the last thing I'd ever want to do is admit it to anyone, including my family."

Samantha's face lost its teasing expression and softened. "Oh, Lin, you don't have to explain. I've been there…trying to deny a part of myself because I didn't want to be considered a freak. I've been watching you for a long time, as long as I've known that you had this same trait. I know it's difficult. And perhaps all this has happened because I'm stronger than I knew, and somehow I've pulled you here, to share this experience with me."

Lindsay frowned a little. "But I thought you said that a book brought you here. Was it that Malory book, the one that you sent to me?"

"Heavens, no," Samantha exclaimed, "I've had that since I was little. I wouldn't send you a book with the deliberate intention of bringing you here. It just happened. Believe me, I was quite shocked when you came parading into the village with the returning travelers. I wasn't able to get to you before you fell asleep, and it's been rather agonizing to think of you all alone and frightened, not knowing how close I was."

Lindsay was completely confused. Aunt Sam seemed to know an awful lot about her, which was certainly gratifying, but at the same time Lin felt that there were things that her aunt just wasn't telling her.

"So you're saying," Lin said slowly, "That this is all real, that we've been dropped into the dark ages because of a magic book." A sudden image popped into her head, of people being carried off into the past by their library books, and she wanted to giggle. "Excuse me if I find that hard to take. Time just can't work that way, and there's no such thing as fairy-tale magic. Maybe it would be better if I just went on believing that this is all a dream and I simply conjured you up with my subconscious."

"I keep forgetting that you're a teenager now," Samantha remarked dryly, "No imagination. But I'm afraid this is as real as our lives back home. I'm a historian, remember? I know that we're in an English castle of the medieval period, and there are plenty of historic events taking place that I know actually occurred. It's actually a scholar's dream come true, to suddenly find yourself living in the midst of your academic specialty."

"How convenient," Lindsay commented, sarcastically, and her aunt gave her an exasperated look.

"I can't supply you with proof, if that's what you're waiting for," she said, sharply.

"I guess I know that," Lindsay replied, with a sigh, "But I wish it could all be neatly tied up, with some tidy little rules about time travel that I could control. I feel helpless."

"I don't know about that," Samantha replied vaguely, almost to herself, "I'm rather afraid to spoil the whole process by analyzing it too much."

Lindsay looked at her sharply. To her, it was beginning to sound as if Aunt Sam did have some secret handbook of time travel, to come and go at will. Was she lying when she said that coming here was all a big accident?

"That's great," Lin said, "But I'd still like to know how I arrived at a place I didn't ask to go to, and I'd like to know what my chances are for reversing the process and going home again."

"There are theories," Samantha remarked, mildly. She leaned over and drew something in the dust: a spiral pattern, like a coiled spring or a Slinky.

"The one I like best is this," she said, sitting back, "Imagine that time is arranged in a spiral. The world is much older than the history of men, so our recorded human history only takes up a few small segments of the coil. So our time, the time you and I belong to, the twentieth century, might occupy a segment directly above the time we're in now, medieval time. Are you still with me?"

Lin nodded, and she continued.

"So we have two sections of the coil, two periods in time directly in line but still separated, of course. Like a spiral staircase, except I'm on a lower stair and you're on an upper stair above me. So then…Imagine that something happens and the spring or coil compresses, just a little. What happens then?"

"Then the segments of the coil would touch," Lin said, picturing the springs of a mattress when you sit on them.

"Right. Now this doesn't happen very often, and when it does there is only the slightest pressure on the tiniest place on the coil. But it seems that the right person might be able to slip from one segment to the other."

"And I suppose that 'the right person' is one who has telepathy." Lin commented.

"Perhaps."

"So you're saying that you came here intentionally!" Lin said, triumphantly.

"I didn't say that," Samantha replied, irritably, "It's just a theory."

"But a while ago you commented that you'd only been 'coming here' for a few months," Lin pressed her, "I take that to mean that you can come and go as you please."

"That's not what I meant," Samantha replied, obviously annoyed, "It just happens. I was here, then one day I was suddenly home again, and then another time I used the book to bring me back again. It doesn't work every time I try."

Her evasiveness was very apparent, and it hurt Lindsay's feelings. If Samantha had found a way to travel back and forth in time, why wasn't she willing to share the secret? Lindsay felt that she might actually be able to enjoy herself here, if she could be assured of going home again when she wanted to.

"Well, I guess that's all there is to it," Lin said finally, with a well-cal-culated wobble in her voice, "But just answer one more question for me: if someday I should ever be magically transported back home again, am I going to find that twenty years have passed, like Rip Van Winkle, and everyone I love will be dead or gone?" Lin was playing for sympathy, but she was a little afraid to hear the answer.

"Oh, Lindsay!" her aunt said, instantly contrite and pulling her into a half hug, "Don't worry about that. I've rarely found more than an hour or two to have passed when I've come back home, and I'm sure it will be the same for you. The transition from one time to another seems to dis-tort clock time quite a bit."

Well, that was comforting, at least. Furthermore, Lindsay had the definite feeling that Aunt Sam was going to be the one to send her home again. And with that reassurance, why not get everything possible out of this amazing adventure?

"Okay, auntie," Lin said flippantly, knowing how Samantha hated being called that, "I guess all that's left is a crash course in this castle and all these people who are supposed to be my family."

Aunt Samantha seemed to be relieved that they had left the topic of time travel logistics, and she laughed as Lindsay stood up and attempted to adjust her long skirts.

"I must teach you how to manage those better," she said, rising and rearranging her own skirts easily, "But as for the workings of this place, let's take a stroll around the village. It's a living history lesson, and we can talk as we walk."

"Great," Lin replied enthusiastically, and they started back toward the garden entrance. It was amazing how much better she felt, now that the fear and the burden of being a stranger in an unknown place had evap-orated. She could relax and maybe enjoy it, and leave the worries to her aunt, since she was obviously keeping a few secrets. As they walked sedately out of the garden, Lindsay never stopped to think about the fact that her once-familiar aunt had actually shown herself to be as much of a stranger to Lin as anyone here in the castle.

CHAPTER 11

Samantha led the way back into the castle and through the great hall where breakfast had been served that morning. She paused in the midst of the now-empty tables.

"This is as good a place to start as any," she said, "You need to know a bit about how rank functions in a castle like this." She gestured toward the tables that stood apart from the others on the raised platforms. "Did you notice this morning that you were eating at a table away from all the others?"

"Mmm-hmm."

"Well, in this place your 'father' is Sir Thomas, a knight and seneschal of this castle. That means he oversees the entire operation of this place. That's why he has a slightly higher position than everyone else."

"Then who sits at the highest table? They must be pretty important...they even get chairs to sit on." Lindsay commented, flippantly.

"That is Sir Robert, the Baron Ellswyth. He is the holder of this castle and has title to all the lands around it. He is a close friend of the king and spends much of his time at court, and only stays here occasionally since his wife died of the smallpox many years ago. His rooms are the floors above ours. He has just one daughter."

"What's smallpox?" Lindsay asked, horrified.

"Rather like chicken pox, only much worse. People either die from it, or end up terribly scarred from the pock marks."

"I guess I did notice some people this morning," Lindsay said, with a shudder, "Like a bad case of acne, but a thousand times worse."

"You can be thankful that they have a vaccine for it in our time," Samantha commented, then frowned, "But if we hear anything about an outbreak, we'll have to get away from here fast. I'd rather catch my diseases in the twentieth century, and have a chance at recovering."

At that point a few servants came in and began to stack the lower tables against the walls until the next mealtime. Samantha and Lindsay made their way back outside.

"Anyway," Samantha continued, "Sir Thomas is the seneschal, so he essentially runs everything. It's a very important post, especially with Sir Robert gone so much of the time. Sir Thomas was only recently knighted, after being a squire for many years."

"I thought men were knighted when they were teenagers."

"Many are. Some can't afford all the trappings, armor and horse and weapons, or have no father to provide it for them. Sir Thomas was knighted and given a small portion of the Baron's lands as a reward for his good service."

Lindsay suddenly remembered all the scathing comments she'd received from the girls she'd ridden through the forest with, about how she was a born peasant. Well, at least it made a little more sense now. Apparently it had been a blow to their pride when she suddenly became a lady instead of a servant's daughter. Lindsay did feel a little hot inside, on Sir Thomas' behalf. She liked him, he seemed as warm and kind as her own dad and she didn't want him to be made fun of by a bunch of snooty girls.

Aunt Sam was looking at her strangely, so Lin put her mind back to the conversation. "So tell me, who else am I supposed to recognize as being a member of my family?" she asked.

"Well, you've met Father, and our mother, of course," Samantha said, with a little smile, "Lady Rosamunde is thrilled at becoming a real lady, but she has decided that it's easier to be an invalid than to perform her proper duties as a lady of the household. Heavens, she might even have to dirty her hands at manual labor! So she stays in bed while Dorothy and I take over all of her responsibilities. Oh, there's also Giles. He's your big brother…you probably saw him at breakfast, too."

"I think I remember him," Lindsay said, thinking back, "Funny, but he didn't greet me at all. Isn't that kind of odd, if I've been away for long time?"

Samantha looked rather nettled. "I have the feeling that Giles isn't overly fond of women, particularly his sisters. I haven't been able to get more than a monosyllable out of him since I've been here. He probably wishes we had been born boys."

Lindsay shrugged. "Oh well. I wouldn't begin to know what to do with a brother, anyway." All this was beginning to bother her, though, having to learn about people who were suddenly supposed to be her family.

"Aunt Sam," she said suddenly, hesitating, "This other Lindsay, the 'real' Lindsay who belongs here…Have you ever seen her?"

Her aunt shook her head. "Remember, I haven't been here that long, and she's been away acquiring her convent education for nearly two years. I was fully expecting to meet her when you arrived instead."

Lindsay frowned. "Well, if I'm here instead, where is she? In my place, back home?" The thought of some medieval Lindsay running around her high school instead of her was enough to make her feel nauseous.

Samantha looked uncomfortable. "I wish I knew the answer to that, Lindsay," she said, pausing before opening the big wooden door to the courtyard. "But remember what I said earlier, about there being a time discrepancy? Perhaps so little time is passing in our world that even if the other Lindsay exists in your place, she won't have time to get into any trouble. Perhaps she didn't even exist here at all, until you came."

Samantha flung open the door and led the way back into the sunshine. Lindsay was still bothered by this whole identity question, but her aunt was clearly finished with the conversation and Lin had to trot to catch up with her.

"Our 'mother' mentioned that you were married," Lin said breathlessly, overtaking Samantha's long strides, "Was she serious?"

Her aunt's face suddenly lit up. "Yes, it's true," she replied, smiling, "Just a month or so ago. His name is Garrick, Sir Garrick."

"You went ahead and married someone you didn't even know?" Lindsay said, her voice rising incredulously, "A perfect stranger?"

"You'll find that most medieval marriages take place between perfect strangers," Samantha responded, dryly. "I was lucky enough to be marrying someone who was quiet and kind and handsome, and I discovered that I liked him very much. It was already agreed upon when I arrived."

Something about that bothered Lindsay. It seemed too convenient. She knew her aunt well enough to know that she'd have found a way out of an arranged marriage, and how would she have gotten to know him well enough in such a short time? Lindsay sighed, and chalked it up to her new list of suspicions about Aunt Samantha. "Well, anyway," she commented, morosely, "You'd never catch me marrying some guy I didn't even know."

Samantha's face suddenly took on a worried expression, but Lindsay didn't notice. She had been distracted by her first up-close-and-personal view of a fully armored knight on his horse. How could a horse support so much sheer weight in metal? Of course, this horse looked like a workhorse, not one of those dainty steeds they always showed in the movies. By the time she turned back to her aunt, she'd forgotten all about the topic of marriage.

"Lindsay," Samantha was saying, rather urgently, "Lin, I don't know how long you're going to be here, but I must tell you that they are arranging a match for you. You're already older than most girls are when they marry, since you went off to be educated. The Baron's own daughter is younger than you, yet she's been betrothed for many years."

"His daughter? Does she live here?'

"She was also at the convent with you, and you rode home together. The Lady Alyce."

Alyce? Oh yes, the beautiful blonde who hadn't seemed too excited about finding a husband. Well, no wonder. Lindsay tried to imagine being married off to a strange man at the tender age of thirteen or so. She herself, at fifteen, had never even been on a date. The idea of being married off was too ludicrous to even think about. Lindsay assured herself that she'd be back home in New Hampshire, going to school and working on the play, long before anyone had a chance to rope her into a wedding.

Lindsay shrugged. "Well, I guess I'll worry about it when the time comes," she said easily.

"We can only hope it never comes at all," Samantha said, sharply. They had reached the heavily guarded gate that led out into the town, and Lindsay suddenly got a whiff of that same stench that had almost knocked her off of her horse the previous day. Just as they were about to pass through the walkway in the immense wall, a small boy came scampering across the cobbles from the castle and rushed up to Samantha.

"Milady," he said, breathlessly, "Mistress Dorothy sent me to find you. The Lady Rosamunde is asking for you."

"Drat that woman!" Samantha said, under her breath so that only Lindsay heard, "Asking for me means that she is demanding my presence in her chamber. Very well," she said to the boy, "Tell her I will attend her momentarily." The boy rushed off again.

She turned to Lindsay. "I'm sorry, Lin, but she does this frequently. Some imagined crisis, I'm sure, but it's not fair to leave it to Dorothy. She has enough to do."

Lindsay was a little disappointed, as she had been curious to see the village and hear more about life here. Samantha studied her, frowning, for a moment, then suddenly smiled.

"I think you could go on by yourself," she suggested. "Everyone knows who you are, so nothing will happen to you if you stay within the town. Don't say anything stupid to give yourself away, and be back for dinner at noontime."

Lindsay was torn between wanting to go but fearing to be alone again in a strange place. How could she avoid saying something stupid when she basically spoke a different language from these people? They might all be speaking English, but Lindsay was definitely speaking 21st century American. But after a brief struggle, her fledgling sense of adventure actually won out. Samantha smiled again, and kissed her cheek. It was certainly disconcerting to know that she was now reading Lin's thoughts as clearly as if she'd spoken.

"Enjoy it all," she whispered in Lin's ear, with a conspirital grin, then straightened up and said in a normal voice, "If you have any difficulties, the tailor on the main street is Dorothy's husband. He can help you…Dorothy says you were great pals when you were a child."

She turned and disappeared back into the courtyard, and Lindsay turned to look out again over the teeming village street. Taking a deep breath for courage, she plunged in.

CHAPTER 12

Lindsay carefully picked her way down the street. It looked even worse down here than it did from horseback, she thought with disgust: filthy and stinking, with frequent mysterious puddles that she didn't dare look at too closely. The houses were so close together that two people could lean out opposite windows and shake hands across the street. Most houses had shops at the street level, tiny dark cubbyholes with all sorts of wares displayed in the open air.

Lindsay wandered along, being jostled by the bustling crowd of people and barely avoiding being trampled by the occasional nobleman or knight on horseback. She tried to find the tailor shop where Samantha said she could find Dorothy's husband, but it was difficult because the shops had no written signs but used symbols instead. A pair of giant scissors seemed to be the obvious choice, and Lindsay peeked into the dark space timidly. A large, ruddy-faced man looked up and then greeted her heartily by name, grinning. Embarrassed, Lindsay mumbled something, smiled weakly, and ducked out again.

Despite the dirt and the smell, it was exhilarating to be here. Lindsay studied the faces of everyone around her, and found to her surprise that they could almost have been the faces of people she'd see at home, cruising the local mall. Same thing, just a whole lot less sanitary, Lindsay thought, and almost giggled aloud. Imagine Mom and Kathi wading through ankle-deep muck to get to a sidewalk sale.

Lindsay admired the brightly-colored fabrics of one shop, and the exotic birds in cages at another stall, temporarily set up in a square because it was market day. There was so much to look at that she wasn't paying much attention to where she was going until a familiar voice brought her up short. She had nearly walked right into a cluster of well-dressed young ladies, complete with servants to hold their horses and carry their purchases. The Ladies Mary and Alyce, and their friend whose name Lindsay had never learned.

"The green one is pretty," Alyce was saying, in her soft voice, pointing at a tray of glittering rings, "And the gold one has a dragon on it, how fanciful! Which do you like, Mary?"

"I don't know...maybe the blue. Or a new necklace, perhaps." Mary said, pretending to sound bored.

Lindsay sidled away, hoping she wouldn't be noticed, but as usual she didn't succeed. Mary chose that precise moment to twitch her skirts further away from the mud, and then glanced straight at Lindsay. A most unladylike sneer spread over her face.

"Well, well, look who came out to play with her peasant friends," she began nastily, "And don't tell me that 'Lady' Lindsay is interested in jewels, when she could be commissioning a suit of armor!" She went off into gales of affected laughter, not noticing that no one else was joining in.

Lady Alyce and the other girl turned, and at least Alyce had the grace to look uncomfortable. Lindsay didn't say anything. How could she? She had no idea what this fight was all about. It all had to do with some other girl, with some other life that she knew nothing about. She certainly couldn't explain that to Mary.

Her lack of response seemed to make Mary angrier, and she took a threatening step toward Lindsay before Alyce caught her by the arm and whispered something into her ear. Whatever it was, it seemed to calm her, and the three of them gracefully mounted their horses with help from their servants, and prepared to leave. At the last moment, however,

Mary wheeled her mare around sharply and pulled up right next to Lindsay, leaning over to hiss malevolently into her face.

"If you think for one minute that I will let you get away with stealing my betrothed husband," she spit, "Just wait and see! No peasant whose father thinks he has rank is going to ruin my plans!"

With her ultimatum delivered, Mary turned the horse again with a savage kick, causing it to founder momentarily in the slippery mud. Its hooves managed to spatter Lindsay with a generous coating of the disgusting street slop. Mary laughed shrilly and forced her way back down the street, leaving Lindsay filthy, bewildered, and more than a little sick from the smell that was now rising from her skirts.

Almost immediately, a small crowd surrounded Lindsay from the nearby shops. One large, pleasant-faced woman produced a wet cloth and wiped Lin's face.

"Oo, that Lady Mary, she's a nasty one, she is," she told Lindsay, in a thick accent, "All she ever thinks about is rank, even though her father gambled away nearly all his money. T'will be hard gettin' a husband for that one, specially with a disposition the likes o' that!"

Everyone laughed heartily, and Lindsay felt a bit better. At least she had a clue now as to what Mary's problem was. Perhaps Samantha could be so kind as to elaborate on the situation, Lindsay thought grimly.

The woman finished dabbing at her face and her gown as best she could, and when Lindsay thanked her she found that her voice had gone all wobbly and she was near tears. After everything that had happened to her in the last few days, Mary's cruelty and the unexpected kindness of the shopkeepers were just too much to handle. Lindsay left as gracefully as she could and then ran blindly down the street, not stopping until she had passed the edge of the village and reached the protective rim of trees that marked the periphery of the forest. She collapsed on a soft patch of mossy grass and gave herself up to crying in earnest, first because of the incident in town and then for homesickness and confusion and worry and everything else.

After a long time, Lindsay snuffled and sat up slowly, wiping at her eyes with her trailing sleeve, which wasn't very clean. She leaned back against a tree and tried to decide if she'd missed dinner at the castle, then listlessly concluded that she didn't care. The only thing she might possibly be hungry for was a hamburger and an extra large order of French fries, but McDonalds didn't seem to have a franchise here yet.

"If you are through sniffling," a voice said suddenly, "Perhaps you would allow me to point out that an insult from the Lady Mary is not worth all the weeping that you are doing."

Lindsay stood up, startled, thinking belatedly of murderers and cut-throats, to say nothing of the humiliation of having someone watch you cry. Leaning casually against a nearby tree was the dark young man whom she had seen at breakfast that morning. It seemed like ages ago.

"It's not just that," she said finally, her voice husky from crying.

He wasn't even looking in her direction but was gazing unconcernedly over the fields. "Then let me guess," he replied insolently, "The travails of homecoming?"

Lindsay sighed, but she was too tired to get defensive at his tone. She was getting tired of meeting people who seemed to hate her for some unknown reason, and she fervently wished that the other Lindsay would come back and fight her own battles.

She took a good look at this young man. His expression was still as sullen as it had been that morning, and his face was very long with a harsh mouth and dark brows that concealed his eyes. He could have been handsome, though, if he looked more pleasant, she thought. As if she'd spoken aloud, he suddenly turned and looked directly at her, and the intense, brilliant blue of his eyes gave her an almost physical shock. They stared at each other for a few seconds before she had to look away.

"How do you know so much about me?" she asked finally, after a few moments. A breeze stirred the trees and cooled her flushed cheeks a little. "About the scene in town, and all that?"

He began to pluck at the bark of the tree he was leaning against. "I have been visiting at the castle for weeks now, and I know that you are Sir Thomas' renegade daughter, freshly returned from a convent education in France. And I was behind you in the street just now. I would have stepped in to defend your honor, but alas, that's not my obligation. I am merely a squire, useful only for polishing armor and lugging things about." This last bit was spoken with unmistakable bitterness.

Oddly enough, it made Lindsay relax a little, to realize that his attitude wasn't due to her. Maybe men got stuck doing things they hated, too. She might be married off to a complete stranger, but he was stuck as a servant to someone else. His broad shoulders and long arms seemed well suited for a sword or bow, even to her inexperienced eyes. She realized she was staring at him again. He was probably the most attractive male she'd ever seen.

Flustered, Lindsay said, "Well, you're stuck as a squire, and I'm being threatened with marriage to a complete stranger, so I don't think either of us can claim to be the more miserable one."

He continued to scowl, then his face suddenly broke into a wry and unexpected grin that totally changed his face.

"I suppose you are right," he conceded, "But you certainly don't sound like other women of my acquaintance, Lady Lindsay. Marriage is the pinnacle of a woman's existence, is it not?"

Lindsay refrained from pointing out that the other women of his acquaintance had probably never been exposed to feminism. Instead, she replied, "This is hardly fair. You know so much about me, but I don't even know your name." No sooner did she say this than she prayed that she wasn't supposed to know him already.

He leaped to attention in front of her and gave a mock bow.

"Excuse me, milady," he said gallantly, "I am Arthur, squire to Sir Cei, who is the betrothed husband of the Lady Alyce and has come to meet his bride."

Lindsay hardly heard the rest of his introduction. She tried to think through what he was telling her. She stood there, gaping at him open-mouthed until he became uncomfortable.

"You're...you're Arthur?" she stammered.

He looked at her with annoyance, his scowl returning, and replied, "Of course I am. Is something wrong? I wasn't aware that I had enough of a reputation to precede me. Have we met before?" This last bit was spoken sarcastically.

"Uh, no," Lindsay temporized, trying to recover, "I...I once knew someone with that name, and it still startles me to hear it, that's all. I'm pleased to meet you, Arthur."

It was a fast lie but it seemed to work, and Arthur's face visibly thawed again. "Well, I'm glad that you don't know me for my faults, as my tutor always warned me," he said, with a small sideways smile, "There are other reputations I would prefer to have."

Before Lindsay had to come up with a reply for that, a bell pealed from the castle walls. Arthur offered her his hand.

"Allow me to make up for my previous lack of chivalry, and escort you safely back for your meal," he said, "Although I must say that you don't look entirely like a lady at the moment."

Lindsay blushed and gave him a withering look, which made him laugh. Ignoring his hand, she brushed ineffectually at her filthy skirts, now dried beyond help.

"Are you sure you want to be seen with me?" she said ruefully, brushing moss out of her hair, "Who knows what this could do to that reputation of yours."

He grinned, and offered his hand again with a gallant gesture that no one else Lindsay's age could have pulled off.

"It makes no difference to me, Milady," he said, "But don't expect me to carry you over the puddles."

Lindsay laughed, and put her hand in his. He tucked it into the crook of his elbow. A little tremor of excitement started somewhere down near her knees and progressed up her spine, as her fingers touched his arm. She wouldn't even allow herself to think that she might well be walking with Arthur, the future king of England.

CHAPTER 13

A trumpeter was announcing the meal when Lindsay and Arthur arrived, breathless, at the door of the great hall. Lindsay had shyly pulled her hand out of his elbow before they entered the courtyard, and once they came into the crowded room Arthur disappeared with nothing more than a half smile in farewell. Lindsay had trouble seeing in the dark room after the bright sunshine outside, and it took her a moment to find Samantha, standing near their table at the head of the room.

"Where have you been?" Samantha hissed at her, as Lindsay reached her side, "I heard some tale about an argument between you and the Lady Mary, right in the main street of the village!"

A page was bringing an elaborate washbowl to the highest table where Lady Alyce was seated beside an older man who must have been the Baron himself. The Baron and his daughter washed their hands, and then Samantha nudged Lindsay to follow her and do the same at a long stone basin with water trickling into it. They dried their hands on a long towel and then sat down at the table with Sir Thomas and Giles.

"The fight in the village was not my fault!" Lindsay whispered hotly to her aunt, "There are a few things you might have told me about, concerning marriages and betrothals and all that!" Her voice had risen angrily, and Samantha hushed her quickly.

"We'll discuss it after dinner," she said, a bit grimly, "And we will also discuss your choice of escorts."

Lindsay blushed. She didn't think anyone had noticed that she and Arthur arrived together. Samantha's tone was awfully ominous. Had she broken some terrible rule about talking to people of the opposite sex? Funny, but plenty of other people seemed to be doing it. Perhaps it was the man himself.

A server placed a round bread bowl in front of Lindsay. "That's your trencher," Samantha said helpfully, under her breath, "It's like a plate. Don't eat it...later on it will be given to the poor."

"Yukk." Lindsay said, "Who'd want to eat someone else's used bread?"

"You'd be surprised." her aunt responded, sadly.

Large wooden platters were being passed up and down the tables, laden with various meats and pastries. Lindsay had no idea what most of it was. Where were the nice, basic fruits and veggies?

"Nobles consider vegetables to be commoners' food," Samantha told her, grinning, "They eat mostly meats, pastries, and sweets. Watch out for the meats, though: they don't have refrigerators, so many times the meat is spoiled and they just cover it up with heavy spices."

"I wish you hadn't told me that," Lindsay said unhappily, gazing at some slices of unidentifiable something on her trencher, "What on earth will I eat?"

"Here." Samantha deftly passed her several platters. "This one is a pudding of wheat and milk. Here's a chicken dish...chicken's a pretty safe bet to be fresh! And take a few of these pastries. That should do."

"Thanks," Lindsay said half sarcastically. What she wouldn't give for a large pepperoni pizza with extra cheese.

They fell silent as they ate. Samantha conversed a bit with her father over the state of the castle and the day's work, but Lindsay ate slowly and thought about Arthur.

How did she know that he was really **the** Arthur, Arthur who became king of England after pulling the sword out of the stone? She had no idea what he looked like. He wasn't like Shakespeare, whose face had adorned the walls of every English classroom she'd sat in since sixth grade. Lindsay figured she'd recognize Shakespeare if she ran into him in a dark alley, but Arthur could be absolutely anyone. Aunt Samantha had told her once that they had never verified that King Arthur actually ever existed, let alone finding a portrait of him.

But it was tantalizing. In the stories, Arthur squires for Cei right up until the day he becomes king, just as this Arthur claimed he did now. And Lindsay couldn't forget the gut feeling she had when he told her his name. He had to be the Arthur, and if he was, then she could get to know him, be his friend, perhaps even help him out of some of the troubles she knew would come to him.

Liar, she told herself, with a little smile. You want to get to know him because he is the most fascinating guy you've ever met in your life, and you don't want to be just his friend.

Well, fat chance of that anyway, given her usual luck in attracting guys. Still, it was a nice dream.

Samantha suddenly looked at her sharply, and Lindsay remembered that her thoughts were no longer her own when her aunt was nearby. Quickly she tried to think about something else...the sour wine in her cup with its cinnamon flavor, or the fact that the floor seemed to be covered with hay, or...She looked up suddenly and found that Arthur was watching her from the opposite side of the room. She met his eyes and he gave her a brisk nod, then returned to his food. From here he didn't look particularly legendary or heroic, just bad-tempered.

The meal ended and they all washed their hands again. Samantha nearly hauled Lindsay out of the room and up the stairs to her tiny bedchamber, where she forced her to sit down on the bed.

"There's no privacy in this damned place," Samantha said, sitting beside her, "But you and I are going to get something straight right away, no matter who overhears. You are not to spend any more time with the young squire Arthur. Do you understand?"

"Why not?" Lindsay asked her, trying to look wide-eyed and innocent.

Samantha looked at her levelly. "You can't fool me, Lindsay, remember? I know you're thinking about him, and I don't think it's wise for you to become too friendly with the man."

"I don't see why I can't," Lindsay said, lightly, "He was kind enough to escort me back here from the edge of the forest. He's very nice. We had a good time."

"The edge of the forest?" her aunt said tightly, "What on earth were you doing there, after I specifically told you not to leave the village? Don't you realize that the forest is a haven for villains and outlaws, and you might have disappeared forever...Or worse?"

"Well, if you had bothered to inform me that I was the sworn enemy of Lady Mary for some reason I know nothing about...something about stealing her husband, for heaven's sakes, then I wouldn't have gotten into a fight with her and ended up running away!" Lindsay said furiously.

Samantha took a deep breath. "Let's calm down," she said, quietly, "Or our mother will be summoning us any moment. The woman can smell conflict, and she loves it."

"Now, about this business with Mary, I am sorry about that. Apparently the man who was negotiating with her father for her hand has called off the deal, since Mary's father lost most of her dowry to gambling. This same man has since approached Sir Thomas about you. I didn't know all this until after you had already gone to the village."

"Well, it was a great introduction to village life," Lindsay said ruefully, studying the stains on her skirts, "I am now intimately acquainted with the mud of the village streets, up close and personal."

"Yes, well, be that as it may," Samantha said, dismissively, "The important issue at hand is Arthur."

"So you also believe that he's the real Arthur, the king of the legends," Lindsay said softly, "And that's why you're warning me away from him."

Samantha eyed her for a moment. "Yes." she said, finally. "I believe he will become King Arthur. I've suspected it for some time, and I won't even allow myself to say hello to him!"

"Whyever not?" Lin asked her curiously.

"Why not? Use your brain, Lindsay! Don't you realize the magnitude of all this? If he is indeed Arthur, future king of Britain, then one wrong word from you, one stupid comment or misguided attempt at helping him could ruin everything! The legends, the history, the whole ideal of Camelot!"

Lindsay sulked a little. "I don't know why I can't be friends with him," she said, "I can keep my mouth shut." She tried to forget that she had considered being able to help him avoid the worst parts of his future.

Samantha sighed. "I might be able to believe that your intentions are good," she said wearily, "And perhaps you could keep from saying the wrong thing for a while. But I know darn well that you aren't just interested in being his friend, and then we'll have the woman in love who has to warn her man about all the pitfalls in his future."

Lindsay's cheeks burned, but she felt defiant. "I will not promise to stay away from him! Think of it as scholarly research…you could be the only scholar to ever prove that Arthur really existed, thanks to me."

"Don't think I haven't thought of that," Samantha said primly, "But I have less faith in my ability to keep my mouth shut than you do, I guess."

Lindsay was not to be deterred. "I'll make a deal with you, Aunt," she said, "I promise never to breathe a word of anything that has to do with the future, if you will let me spend time with Arthur."

Samantha studied her for a moment, then sighed. "I never suspected you could be so determined," she said, "But I can see it's hopeless and I'm too tired to fight with you any more today. So I'll agree to the deal, but only temporarily. I'll be watching you closely, my girl. And remember: in this time and place, a girl like you doesn't chase a man like Arthur. You'll only enjoy more of his company if he so wants it."

Lindsay grinned at her. "Well, here's hoping," she said, and Samantha smiled back in spite of herself. Then she rose and straightened her skirts.

"Come along now, Lindsay. It's time you participated in the customary occupation of the ladies of this castle. But after you change that skirt." Then she led the way out of the room and up the stairs to a large, comfortable room that she called the solar. It was like a big living room or parlor, with huge windows overlooking the garden, lit by the warm autumn sunshine. A dozen or so women were busily absorbed in needlework and gossip, and they all greeted Samantha and Lindsay and made places for them.

Lindsay looked at the cloth and yarns in front of her rather distastefully, and whispered to Samantha, "I'd rather read a good book. Where's the library?"

"Hush!" Samantha admonished her, pretending to be cross but smiling a little. Lindsay sighed. She had been forced to learn embroidery in junior high home-ec class, so she scrounged for a needle and some yarn and tried her hand at it. It wasn't bad, actually, sort of a soothing occupation, and she was pleased with her efforts until she happened to notice that there was a little girl nearby, only four or five years old, whose work was about twice as good as Lindsay's. Somewhat deflated, she kept working but devoted her thoughts to Arthur. The question of how long she would be here, in this time and place, had a new significance now that she'd met him. It was hard to believe that she had only been here for two days. It was actually beginning to feel homelike.

Chapter 14

The days passed, and gradually Lindsay stopped waking up each morning expecting to be back home in New Hampshire. She began to adjust to the routine of life in the castle, spending much of her time with Samantha and learning something about the way the huge household was run. Most afternoons were spent in the solar, doing endless needlework with the other women. That was probably the most tedious part of the day, and Lindsay had to admit that she wasn't getting any better at it, but she liked listening to all the castle gossip.

Most afternoons, the main topic was weddings. There seemed to be a bumper crop of marriageable females that year, and everyone had an opinion about who should marry whom. Lady Alyce's wedding was also being planned, with a grand ceremony and feasting and entertainment, and it sounded like the social event of the season.

"Of course, Alyce will have to manage that huge household when Sir Cei takes her home to his father's holding, and there hasn't been a woman to run things in that castle since Sir Ector's wife died." one of the women was saying, "But Alyce has been well taught."

"Yes," agreed another, "Sir Cei certainly had his wits about him when he chose his bride! Comely and sensible, that's the perfect combination."

"And he makes a worthy suitor for our Alyce," sighed a third woman.

"I hear that Sir Cedric is an impressive suitor," someone said archly, "At least, the Lady Mary was quite taken with him."

"We shouldn't speak lightly of such matters," an older woman said severely, "It is not the poor child's fault that her father has lost her dowry money to gaming, and has ruined her marriage prospects."

"Well, Sir Cedric certainly wasted no time in attempting to forge a more advantageous alliance," the first woman replied, giving Lindsay a sidelong glance.

Samantha rose suddenly. "Lindsay," she said smoothly, "I believe it is time that we looked in on our lady mother. If you will all excuse us?" Lindsay stood up reluctantly, her ears nearly burning with curiosity, and followed her out the door. She was dying to know the whole story behind this business of Mary's future husband, but she could tell by the set of Samantha's mouth that she was not pleased with the whole conversation. Thinking they were out of earshot of the solar, Lindsay couldn't keep still.

"I think it's time you explained just what's going on with all this marriage stuff," she said, crossly, nearly stumbling down the stairs as she tried to keep up with Samantha.

"Shh...Samantha looked even more annoyed. "Your voice carries too well, Lindsay, and there's enough gossip about all this as it is." She led the way out through the kitchens and into the garden where the herbs and household vegetables were grown. They steered away from the vicinity of the servants.

"I'm beginning to see a comparison between walking in the garden for privacy, and locking yourself in the bathroom, like we did at home," Lindsay grumbled, following along, "But what will you do in the winter?"

"Let's hope we won't have to find out," Samantha replied grimly, "We'll stroll along like two well-bred women and I'll tell you the entire story of the fickle Sir Cedric. It seems to be the gossip topic of the month, and you're bound to be hearing more about it anyway."

"Lady Mary was to be betrothed to Sir Cedric. He has a good-sized holding of land and is a very worthy match, so the girl was going to do quite well with the marriage. Until a few months ago, when for some unknown reason her father entered into a rather drastic bout of gambling and managed to lose most of his money and holdings. So without much of a dowry and little else to offer, Lady Mary is no longer much of a marriage prospect, and Sir Cedric has withdrawn his suit for her hand."

"Wow," Lindsay said finally, with feeling, "I suppose it wasn't a love match, but still…Poor Mary. I guess I'd feel a little sour, too, if it happened to me. But how do I fit into all this?"

Aunt Sam sighed. "Because Sir Cedric has now gone to your father and asked that a marriage be arranged between the two of you."

"Oh, no!" Lindsay cried, coming to a complete standstill, "No wonder she hates me. I'm surprised she didn't throw me into a puddle. So now I'm up for grabs, like a piece of property?"

Samantha took her elbow and forced her to continue walking. "You must first try to understand what a wonderful match this is in Father's eyes, to marry you off to someone as successful as Sir Cedric. And since you returned from the convent, it appears that you've been quite a bit more biddable and ladylike than the Lindsay who left several years ago. He probably wants you settled before you begin to act up again!"

"Doesn't he even have to ask my opinion on the subject?" Lindsay said, depressed.

Samantha gave her a humorless grin. "He doesn't even have to tell you about it until he leads you to the altar," she said. "You should realize by now that life here doesn't offer a woman very many choices."

"So what happens now?" Lindsay said, uneasily, "I'm not ready to leave here yet, even if I could. I haven't met your husband, or seen any jousting, or even completely explored the castle…" Or seen Arthur again, except from afar, she added silently.

"But we don't want you to be here when the day arrives for your marriage," Samantha said clearly, as if Lindsay was a child, "Still, we have some time. There are many details to work out in a betrothal, it's more of a business deal than an engagement. And then there'll be more time before the wedding actually takes place, months perhaps. We'll just have to play along and hope you'll return home before then. Meanwhile, do your best to ignore the gossip. And for heaven's sake, stay out of Mary's way!"

Lindsay thought to herself that Samantha didn't seem all that worried about getting her out of the way when the time came, which just added to her private theory that Aunt Sam could send her home any time she pleased. A few days before the wedding and zap! Lindsay would be magically transported safely back to the twenty first century. Well, that was fine with her. Lindsay wasn't ready to leave, not a bit. Every morning when she awoke, it was just slightly more difficult to conjure up her life at home, her friends, school…At times, even her family's faces dimmed a little, overshadowed by those here at the castle. Imperceptibly, her attachment to this life was growing. Only Aunt Sam's presence reminded her of home, but even then whole days could pass in which they never mentioned any other life than this one.

Like the ruby slippers in Oz, Aunt Sam had probably been able to send her home since the very first day, Lindsay thought to herself reassuringly. So she put all the wedding business out of her mind for the moment, and continued to enjoy herself.

After dinner, as Lindsay was heading for the garden for a few last minutes of fresh air, someone tapped her on the shoulder. She turned, startled, and it was Arthur, his dark face glimmering with an unaccustomed smile.

"Lady Lindsay," he said, with an exaggerated bow that was still graceful, "I would like to request the honor of your companionship tomorrow for riding."

"Riding?" Lindsay said, dumbly, "Sure, I guess…l mean, yes, I'd like that."

Arthur smiled again, and Lindsay's heart was thumping as his blue eyes met hers directly. "I thought perhaps you might appreciate a ride through the meadows and along the forest under more auspicious circumstances," he said, and she blushed. "We'll go out early…I'll see that your horse is brought around right after breakfast, so we can avoid attracting any unwanted company."

Lindsay nodded, feeling like she was incapable of talking coherently. How great could it get? Arthur, Lindsay, and the countryside. At that, Arthur melted back into the crowd of diners leaving the hall, and Lindsay continued happily out the door when Samantha caught up with her.

Lindsay steeled herself for a lecture on Arthur, but Samantha's face was wreathed in smiles. "Lin!" she said, happily, "I've just received news that Garrick will be returning tomorrow!"

"Your husband?" Lin asked, and she nodded. "That's great! I'll get to meet him!"

It seemed a little weird to see Samantha so excited about a guy she'd been forced to marry in a supposedly loveless match, Lindsay thought to herself, but she just filed that suspicion away for future reference.

"I'd appreciate it if you could take over some of my duties tomorrow," Samantha said softly, "Just to help out Dorothy, and give me a little extra time to myself."

"Sure," Lindsay replied, still amazed by her giddiness. She'd never imagined her scholarly, sophisticated aunt acting like this. "I'm going riding early in the morning, but I'll help after that."

That brought her back to earth. "Riding?" she questioned, "With whom? Some of the ladies?"

"Arthur," Lindsay replied, lightly.

Samantha gave her customary sharp sigh. "And here I was, beginning to think that perhaps that was just a one-time encounter. Need I remind you that not only are you playing with fire where Arthur himself is concerned, but you are now practically engaged as well? Being seen in the company of another man will only feed the gossip."

"Say what you want, Auntie," Lin replied maddeningly, "I don't care. I'm going no matter what you say."

They stared at each other for a few moments in a battle of wills, and surprisingly enough it was Samantha who looked away first.

"In that case," she said, tiredly, "I hope it's worth it."

CHAPTER 15

Lindsay had never been very good at primping. She always envied those girls who could do their hair perfectly and look so well put-together. She could never quite pull it off, and now, without a nicely lit bathroom mirror and a curling iron, it was even worse. Still, by the time she was ready to go down to breakfast the next morning, she felt fairly attractive. Her hair was neatly braided and she was wearing a tunic and gown in shades of emerald green, her favorite color.

"Good morning, Lindsay," Dorothy said cheerfully, bustling in while Lindsay took one last look at herself in her inadequate mirror. Then she frowned. "I've been meaning to ask you, child, why aren't you wearing any of your other jewels? Now that the emerald suits you, you should be wearing them all. Don't tell me they were misplaced on the journey home..." Worry creased her forehead and she began rummaging through Lin's chest of clothing.

"More jewels?" Lindsay squeaked.

"Ah, here they are," Dorothy said, with relief. She held a small, carved wooden box and opened it as she walked over to Lindsay. "Here, this will suit that gown quite nicely."

She held out a beautiful golden necklace set with several small, perfect rubies. It was even more elaborate than the necklace Lindsay had worn since the first day in the castle, and which was still under her dress. The stones glimmered as Dorothy stood behind Lindsay, fastening it around her neck and looking at the result with satisfaction. "Perfect," she said, "You're looking quite comely, my girl."

Lindsay could hardly speak. The gorgeous necklace shone softly against the cloth of her dress. "It's beautiful," she sighed.

Dorothy looked at her oddly. "Of course it is," she remarked, "You've been wearing it since you were twelve."

Lindsay blushed, and covered it up by looking into the wooden box with interest. Several brooches, earrings, and another necklace, most of them set with jewels. Her mother would have a fit. She wouldn't even let Lin have tiny diamond earrings yet.

They went down to breakfast, Lindsay's stomach churning nervously. She could see Arthur and Cei eating together and she could hardly swallow her own food. It seemed like a lifetime before the meal was over and she could go out into the courtyard.

The cool morning air just bordered on chilly and Lindsay was glad that she'd grabbed a cloak to wear over her shoulders. Arthur was waiting with one of the small stable lads, who held a pretty chestnut-colored mare for Lin to ride.

"No one seemed to be able to tell me which horse was yours" Arthur explained, "You don't seem to have one yet, since you returned, so I took the liberty of choosing this one."

"She's lovely," Lindsay replied, nervously, and accepted the help of the boy in getting onto her horse's back. Sixth-grade summer camp had never addressed the problem of getting onto a horse gracefully when you were wearing long skirts. To say nothing of balancing elegantly in a sidesaddle…it was the most awkward position Lindsay had ever tried, and she only prayed that she might not fall off the horse in a graceless heap, right under Arthur's nose.

They rode out of the courtyard and down the main street, already bustling with the activity of the day as the peasants headed to the fields to harvest the last of their crops. They followed the road from the village gates until they reached the unplanted meadows that skirted the edges of the forest.

Lindsay felt tongue-tied with shyness. She kept glancing sideways at Arthur from under her eyelashes. He was so at ease on his horse, riding as if held been born to, his face relaxed and almost smiling. As if held felt her gaze, he turned toward her and smiled.

"It's so peaceful here," he remarked, "At times the endless bustle and crowds of the town and the castle are enough to nearly drive me mad, and then I come out here riding or hawking, just to be alone."

"Yes," Lindsay replied, noticing that the autumn colors were beginning to fade on the trees, and the grass was crisp with traces of frost. "I'm not looking forward to being cooped up all winter."

Arthur didn't reply, and they continued on in silence, the horses at an easy walking pace. Lindsay began to wonder of Arthur was finding her company to be disappointing. She felt like a lump, balanced there on her horse with the beginnings of a backache from the unaccustomed posture.

Curiously, it suddenly occurred to her that perhaps she could get some sort of glimmering as to just what Arthur was thinking. She'd never been tempted to try this on a guy before, perhaps being afraid of what she'd hear, but she was feeling rather desperate. She didn't want to blow it with him. Lindsay closed her eyes for a moment and tried to focus on the man beside her.

Odd...nothing at all. That had never happened before. Usually she could get at least a few snippets of thought when she deliberately tried, but this was like meeting the resistance of a velvet-black wall. Arthur rode on, unperturbed, so it couldn't be that he was blocking her, as Aunt Sam could.

They passed a man working in a nearby field, and Lindsay focused on him, instead. It was a bit better...he was worried about the harvest, and having enough for his family to eat that winter...and yet Lindsay had to concentrate because the man's thoughts seemed somehow muted to her. She made a note to ask Samantha about it.

"Let's ride into the forest a bit," Arthur said easily, turning his horse onto an obvious path, "I think we'll be safe enough if we don't go far."

"Safe from whom?"

"Oh, the usual criminals…Cutthroats, thieves, beggars, outlaws." Arthur said loftily, and Lin giggled.

"It sounds like you're personally acquainted with them," she teased, "I suppose you'll tell me next that you're a great friend of Robin Hood."

"Who?" he said blankly, and Lin sighed.

"No one," she said quickly. "A story I heard in the convent."

The forest was even cooler and Lin shivered a bit in her woolen cloak. Finally Arthur pulled his horse up and stopped.

"This is far enough," he said reluctantly, "I won't risk taking a lady any further. Would you like to stretch your legs for a moment?"

"Definitely," Lindsay said, with feeling, and slid ungracefully off her horse. Her back was killing her and one leg was nearly asleep. She nearly fell over when she hit the ground, and steadied herself by clutching the saddle. When she looked up again, Arthur was laughing at her.

"What's so funny?" she demanded indignantly, and then had to smile. She was balanced on one leg, practically hanging off the horse's neck. "Oh…I'm so used to riding the regular way, I just can't seem to get the hang of this sidesaddle business."

"It does look quite uncomfortable," Arthur said, sympathetically, "Let me tether your horse, and we'll sit for a few minutes." He draped the horses' reins over a nearby branch, and dusted off a boulder for Lin to sit on. It was such a relief to sit straight. She only wished she could think of a discreet way to sit cross-legged.

Arthur sat down beside her, and Lindsay suddenly felt like every nerve in her body was individually aware of his nearness.

"I used to spend most of my free time in the forest," Arthur said, gazing up at the trees and the drifting leaves that fell from their branches, "I grew up in Sir Ector's castle, he's Cei's father. I was a fosterling, like most children, but I had no other home of my own, and no parents."

"Were you and Cei friends?" Lin asked, softly.

"Oh yes, great friends. We were nearly brothers, and we did our lessons together and played together and concocted mischief together. I thought it would always be that way, until the day when Cei was knighted and I became nothing more than his squire."

"How does he treat you now?" Lindsay asked, idly plucking at the moss that grew on her boulder.

"Oh, well enough, I suppose," Arthur said, standing up and pacing restlessly, "But it's difficult, after being treated as his equal for so long, to accept that I must be his servant now."

"Forever?"

"Perhaps. Or perhaps I might earn my own knighthood someday, as a soldier to some lord or baron. Not as a birthright, as in Cei's situation."

Lindsay tried to imagine Arthur as a soldier, fighting nameless in a nameless battle. It was hard to listen to all of this, when she knew so well the glory and the legends that awaited him.

"And you, milady?" Arthur said suddenly, ceasing his pacing and leaning on a nearby branch, "How did Lady Lindsay arrive at such a great age without being married?"

Lindsay's face burned with sudden irritation. "Marriage. I am everlastingly sick of the word!"

Arthur was taken aback for a moment, then laughed. "I forgot who I was speaking to," he said. "How is it that you should not want to be married?"

Lindsay panicked a little. How could she hope to explain it to him? She searched desperately for some tidbit, something she'd been told about the other Lindsay that could help her out.

"Well, I've spent my whole life in this castle," she said carefully, after a moment, "And as a girl, I was never allowed to do what I wanted to: riding, hawking, just being free. And then they send me off to a convent for an education, and suddenly when I return I've become a piece of goods to be bargained away to the highest bidder. Why can't I have a life of my own, without depending on marriage?"

"Because women need to be taken care of," Arthur replied, in surprise, "A noblewoman such as yourself certainly does not labor in the fields or run a stall at the marketplace."

Lindsay sighed. It was hopeless to explain. The gulf between his world and hers was too great.

"So when you were little they forced you into that ladylike mold, despite what you wanted," Arthur remarked casually, shredding bark off the branch.

"Well, yes, I suppose."

"Liar!" Arthur pounced, turning to her with a triumphant smirk, "I've heard plenty of stories about you, Milady Lindsay, running wild around the castle and the village because you were the youngest and your father was too soft-hearted to rein you in. It made you quite a favorite in the town, and they had plenty of stories to tell when they heard you were coming home. I was actually quite curious to see you."

Lindsay flushed fiercely, and turned away, her lips pressed together angrily. She disliked being trapped, especially when she was already playing such a delicate game of trying to be someone she was not, twenty-four hours a day. She could feel Arthur watching her, and finally he leaned over and took her chin in his hand, forcing her to look at him.

"You're not telling me the truth about many things," he said thoughtfully, "And I don't know why. It's intriguing. What are you hiding?"

"Nothing," she replied shortly, jerking her chin away. He continued to study her for another moment, then appeared to change the subject.

"Cei and the Lady Alyce will be marrying in a few weeks' time," he remarked, "And then I'll be returning home with them."

"I know," Lindsay said, relieved to be on another topic, "It's all the ladies can talk about. Well, nearly all."

"It bothers me," Arthur said, after a pause, "Once again, Cei goes on with his life while I'll still be stuck in the same position, waiting on him. Actually, it infuriates me."

"How do you think I feel?" Lindsay burst out, leaping to her feet, "Apparently I'm going to be married off to some man I've barely glimpsed, some Sir Cedric. He's probably forty years old and completely repulsive!"

"He's not," Arthur replied, rather absently, "I've seen him. He's quite acceptable, actually, and his holdings are respectable. You'll be doing better than many young ladies. Why does it bother you so much?"

"It's just not the way I want my marriage to be," Lindsay said truthfully, knowing she was taking a risk in trying to explain it, "I always imagined that I would marry someone whom I chose, someone I could talk to and enjoy being with. Someone I loved."

She regretted this as soon as she said it. Obviously love and marriage were two separate things here, although they might happen together from sheer luck once in a while.

Arthur circled the tree he was leaning on until he was standing in front of Lindsay. He studied her with that penetrating gaze of his, until she squirmed.

"You know," he said finally, "At times I have thought that I would like marriage to be that way myself."

Lindsay frowned, wondering if he was making fun of her, but then he leaned over with excruciating slowness and kissed her, gently at first and then more enthusiastically as he took her into his arms and drew her closer.

All sorts of warnings were going off in Lindsay's brain: bits of Aunt Sam's lecture, fear of being alone in the forest with him and no one else around, and that maddening thrill that ran up her spine and drowned out everything else. Her first kiss. And who would ever believe this?

Finally Arthur drew back, taking both of her hands in his and smiling. "And is that how you imagined being kissed?" he said, teasingly.

Lindsay blushed. "No," she said, a bit breathlessly, "I never imagined it like this!"

CHAPTER 16

Lindsay would have been perfectly happy to stay in the forest with Arthur forever, but unfortunately all too soon they had to return to the castle for the midday meal. They mounted their horses and returned to the village at a rather leisurely pace, laughing and talking, until they were in the midst of the village crowds once again.

The groom appeared as soon as they entered the courtyard, to take the horses back to the stable. Lindsay knew that she shouldn't let anyone see how she felt about Arthur, and how things were between them, but when he helped her down from her horse they gazed at each other for a moment in a rather obvious way. Lindsay knew she was starry-eyed and giddy, but for the first time in her life (or since she was twelve and discovered boys, which amounted to pretty much the same thing), someone liked her and was attracted to **her**, not Andrea or Kathi or Chris. And she had actually been kissed for the first time, those tired old party games of spin-the-bottle notwithstanding. Too bad that no one at home would ever be able to admire Arthur.

Lindsay was so wrapped up in her little pink clouds of romance that she never even noticed a cluster of men who were standing near the doorway. One of them glanced at her, then stared more intently at Arthur beside her, before flushing an angry red and speaking to his companions in an irate undertone.

"Trouble." Arthur said, speaking softly into her ear, "That is the illustrious Sir Cedric, and I don't think he was very pleased to see you in my company."

Lindsay glanced back, hoping to catch a glimpse of the man it seemed she was intended to marry, but the crowd had already swallowed him up. She shrugged, and turned around again.

"I don't care," she said recklessly, "I have no intention of marrying him anyway." This sounded very fine and bold to say out loud, but Arthur looked somewhat startled. Lindsay flashed him a dazzling smile before she threaded her way through the other tables to her own. Maybe those flirtation genes her sisters seemed to possess had just been lurking below the surface of her own personality.

Arthur looked a bit disconcerted and went to his own place without returning the smile. Lindsay watched him for a moment and then sat down, so preoccupied that at first she didn't even notice the new face at the table.

"Lindsay," Samantha said finally, clearing her throat gently, "I would like you to meet my husband, Sir Garrick. Garrick, this is my sister Lindsay."

Lindsay wasn't sure what she was supposed to do. Shake hands? Get up and curtsey? Sir Garrick, however, just nodded, so she nodded back and murmured that she was honored, or something dumb like that. He was very handsome, fair-haired, and blue-eyed, and he looked about nineteen. He seemed to be quite fond of Samantha, smiling at her in a way that spoke of shared secrets. Samantha actually seemed to be in the middle of the same rosy glow that Lindsay herself was wallowing in. Lin became so involved in watching them, in between sneaking furtive glances at Arthur, that dinner passed quickly and she couldn't remember what she'd eaten. Hopefully it wasn't something rotten.

She rose from the table just as Sir Cedric appeared at her father's elbow and began discussing something with him in the same angry tone. They were both watching her as she lingered in the doorway before going up to the solar, pausing to see Arthur and Cei leave the hall together. Sir Cedric finished his tirade and departed, and Father rose wearily and headed in Lindsay's direction.

"Daughter, a word with you please," he said quietly, taking her by the elbow and steering her into his little office near the kitchen.

He sat down behind his worktable, leaving Lindsay to stand awkwardly in front of him, fidgeting and playing nervously with her skirt.

"I did not think I would need to speak of this just yet," Sir Thomas began, "But since Sir Cedric has found it necessary to inform me of your recent activities, it leaves me no choice."

Lindsay shifted her weight from one foot to the other. What code of behavior had she broken? It had been a relatively harmless morning with Arthur, and since no one had told her that she was officially engaged to Sir Cedric, what was the problem?

"Lindsay," her father continued, with an edge to his voice as he tried to get her wandering attention back, "Something very fortunate has befallen you. I had always hoped to make a good marriage for you, but this exceeds my expectations. Sir Cedric has asked for your hand, and he and I have worked out a mutually satisfactory arrangement. Everything is now set for a formal betrothal. What do you say, child?"

Lindsay gaped at him. So the gossip was all true, and she had been bargained over and sold, like a piece of goods in a shop! It was happening much too quickly...Samantha had said they would have more time!

"I know this comes as a surprise, my dear," Sir Thomas said benevolently. Was he dense? Lin wondered, wanting to laugh. Didn't he know it had been a major topic of discussion all over the castle for weeks now?

"Sir Cedric wanted to settle things quickly," her father was saying, "So from this point forward you must consider yourself to be engaged, which brings us to the other issue at hand. Cedric tells me that you came in to dinner with young Cei's squire, looking as if you'd been off cavorting in the woods like a serving wench. I never expected this sort of thing to become a problem with you, Lindsay, which is why I didn't speak earlier, but I shouldn't need to tell you that you must be more circumspect now."

"But Father!" Lindsay said, finding her voice at last, "I don't want to marry this Sir Cedric! I've never even met the man, and he's old! And Arthur...well, Arthur and I have an...an affection for each other..." Her words trailed off as Sir Thomas' face darkened with anger.

"Arthur?" he thundered, "A young squire with nothing to his name, and hardly a name of his own, at that? An orphaned fosterling of Sir Ector's. You don't seem to understand, my girl. You have been promised to Sir Cedric, and I do not want to see you with this Arthur again! I have been lenient with you in the past, but I will stand firm on this. You will never have a better marriage opportunity than this, and I will not allow you to lose it through childish impetuosity!"

If you only knew, Lindsay cried out inwardly, If you only knew that someday he will be High King of Britain, you'd give us your blessing in an instant.

"The betrothal will take place in a week's time," her father said firmly, rising from his chair, "And I will have no further nonsense from you. Believe me, someday you will thank me."

The adult litany. It didn't matter what century you lived in, adults always believed they knew what was right for you.

"I doubt that," Lindsay replied nastily, and fled, her head whirling. As usual, she would have given almost anything for a room of her own and a door that locked, but she had to make do with the kitchen gardens again. She paced the gravel paths, trying to calm down and think clearly.

This betrothal meant two things: either she would have to return to her own time much more quickly than she really wanted to, or she would have to find a way to get out of her marriage to Cedric. If marriage were such an issue, she would marry Arthur. Leaving now would mean never seeing him again. Why not marry him? Then, once he was king, everyone would be thrilled that she'd chosen him. Of course, it occurred to her that all they'd shared so far was a few kisses. Other girls she knew kissed a different guy at every school dance and then forgot about it the next day. Lindsay wondered, with a frown, if Arthur was more accomplished at affairs of the heart than he appeared to be. Lindsay knew that the idea of marrying him was jumping to incredible conclusions, but during the morning she had decided that she was in love with him and she would marry him. How weird, to be fifteen years old and seriously thinking about marrying! It would seem horrible at home, but was natural here, where Lindsay was practically an old maid.

She wished she could talk to Aunt Sam, but she was probably occupied with Sir Garrick. She would have to deal with it on her own anyway, since Samantha was so disapproving of her having anything to do with Arthur. Lindsay needed a plan, and she needed to talk to Arthur. He would know what to do, she thought, with the supreme confidence of someone madly in love. She would find him after the evening meal, and he would help her work it out.

With that resolved, Lindsay blew the wisps of hair out of her eyes and went inside to find Dorothy. She spent a quiet afternoon in the solar and helping Dorothy with her tasks, letting the rest of the castle's business swirl around her.

CHAPTER 17

The evening meal seemed to go on forever. Lindsay fidgeted and picked at her food even more than usual. All she could think about was being alone with Arthur, and working out some sort of a plan to get her out of her impending betrothal. She wanted to stay with Arthur and that ruled out a sudden return to her own time, although she was sure that was what Aunt Sam had in mind.

Samantha was still quite preoccupied with her husband...how odd that sounded to Lindsay, after years and years of considering her aunt to be a confirmed spinster. They disappeared to their chambers as soon as the meal was over. Father sat with Giles, speaking to him in a low, serious tone while Giles eyed Lindsay sharply. Unfortunately, she was so busy scanning the hall for Arthur that she didn't notice their conversation.

Thankfully the hall began to clear, and Lindsay slipped out into the courtyard. Arthur was standing with a group of men, listening to Cei and the others, and laughing. She sidled up beside him and tugged at his sleeve.

"Arthur," she said, softly, "Can I talk to you for a minute? It's important."

Arthur looked startled, then he put an arm around her waist and guided her away from the group of men, who were grinning and making ribald comments.

"This won't do much for your reputation, you know," Arthur said wryly, as they found their way into the gardens. Lindsay thought to herself that she would never think of gardens the same way again, for the rest of her life. They found a stone bench to sit on and Lindsay smoothed her skirts, surprised to find that her hands were shaking.

"What is it, Lindsay?" Arthur said, with just a trace of annoyance in his voice, "I was just about to join Cei in some gaming."

"It's...it's..." Lindsay stuttered awkwardly, taken aback by his tone, "My father called me into his office today. I am to be formally betrothed to Sir Cedric."

"Any other woman would ask for my congratulations," Arthur said, taking her hand and squeezing it gently, "But I gather that you are not like other women and this does not suit you."

He seemed rather offhand. Shouldn't he be pledging his love for her and vowing not to let any other man have her? Lindsay thought, disappointed.

"So what am I going to do?" she asked him, through clenched teeth.

"Do?" Arthur repeated, blankly, "Why, you will marry him, of course. Your father has willed it so."

Lindsay closed her eyes for a moment and reminded herself that Arthur had never been exposed to twenty-first century attitudes.

"I will not marry some old man who I have never met and most certainly do not love," she said patiently, as if speaking to a child, "I will not! And I was hoping that perhaps you might have some sort of suggestion as to how I could get out of it."

"I have never met a woman who actually refused a good match," Arthur said, looking at Lindsay as if she was a great curiosity. Lindsay grew more and more impatient. Why wasn't he offering to sweep her off her feet and carry her away on his horse, like a proper chivalrous knight?

"It looks like I'm going to have to spell this out myself," she said, under her breath, and then, "Arthur, I want to leave here, to run away from this place. And I want you to come with me. I...I love you."

His face registered incredible shock, and Lindsay suddenly felt uneasy. Had she made a mistake and gone too far? Didn't men and women ever run off together for love, even in this time and place?

"Wouldn't you like to get out from under Cei's thumb?" she said, more gently, "Wouldn't you like to be your own man, live your own life? This is your chance! We both want to get away. We could start a new life together."

"Marriage?" he questioned her, suddenly.

"Eventually," Lindsay said easily, "When we have the chance."

Arthur looked quite scandalized, and again Lindsay nearly snorted from frustration at the difference between their two cultures. Apparently men here could fool around with the peasant girls, but a lady must be married first.

"I have no holdings, no title," Arthur said thoughtfully, "And if we run away there will be no dowry from your father. How do you propose to survive? I may be able to hire myself to another lord as a mercenary, but where will you live if I am off fighting his battles?"

Lindsay suddenly felt quite tired. "I don't know," she said wearily, slumping a little, "I suppose we could worry about it as we went along. I just know that I would rather be anywhere with you, than comfortably married off to Sir Cedric." She looked down at the ground.

Arthur was silent for a moment, and then he put his hand under her chin and forced her to look at him. He kissed her slowly.

"I don't know," he said, troubled, "I must be honest and tell you that I have yet to think much on my feelings for you. I don't usually kiss fair ladies in the forest, but I have kissed a few elsewhere, and they don't ever propose marriage after."

If I could only tell you what a favor you'd be doing for me and for yourself if you married me, Lindsay thought. She had no problem with the idea of being Queen of Britain, and she could prevent all that nasty business with Guinever. It didn't occur to her that running off with Arthur might change destiny to the point where he might never become king.

Finally Arthur sighed, taking Lindsay's hand again. "I must think on this," he said. "If it is so important to you, to escape this betrothal, then perhaps there is a way. Sir Ector might even keep me on…or recommend my service to another. It would be exciting to face the world as my own man." His eyes got a faraway look, and Lindsay smiled, knowing she had him closer to being convinced.

"Meet me in the garden again tomorrow evening," she said softly, "Tell me then what you have decided, and we can make our plans." She kissed him shyly on the cheek. He nodded, then reached for her, and kissed her in return, on the lips this time and a trifle more ardently than before.

"Lindsay!" a voice thundered, and they drew apart quickly as Giles appeared through the dusk. His dark face was contorted with anger, and Lindsay was suddenly afraid as he came forward and grabbed her elbow so viciously that she gasped in pain.

"Father warned me that I might find you in some dark corner with this…this squire," he spat out, sneering at Arthur, "Get to your room, girl, and don't let me see you with him again. Anywhere!" Giles shoved Lindsay toward the gate, and she went reluctantly, glancing back at the two men.

"Keep your distance from my sister, squire," he said to Arthur, in a menacing tone, "She's been promised to another man. Someone worthy of her rank."

Lindsay could barely see Arthur's face, but he looked remarkably composed, even insolent. For a moment she was afraid of what he might say to taunt Giles, perhaps spoiling their plans, but he merely gave Giles an infuriating half-smile and sauntered off. Lindsay was slightly disappointed that he didn't put on some sort of knightly stand on her behalf, but Giles was much taller and heavier than he and not a good choice for a fistfight.

Giles gave an inarticulate snarl, and then caught up with Lindsay. Grabbing her elbow again, he hustled her inside. She had to concentrate on negotiating the steps to her room as he hauled her along, not daring to stumble lest he should decide to drag her. So she only half heard his continuous lecture until he nearly threw her onto her face on the floor of her room.

"Father has instructed me to watch you, little sister," he said, turning to leave, "And I intend to watch you very closely indeed, now that I know you're not the little mouse you were pretending to be." With that, he went back downstairs before Lindsay could come up with a sufficiently scathing reply. Samantha was right: he did hate them.

There didn't seem to be anything else to do except go to bed. As she pulled up her covers, Lindsay wished once again that Arthur had acted a bit more nobly when Giles found them, instead of smirking. Why hadn't he defended her honor? And why hadn't he said that he loved her, too? It was frustrating. He just wouldn't act like her ideal of a heroic knight.

She sighed, and flopped over onto her stomach to go to sleep. She'd forgotten, somehow, that she was dealing with a very real Arthur, a boy not much older than herself, confused and discontent. He was a real person now, not a mythic king. But she had set things in motion and all she could do now was continue with her plans. Without realizing it, though, Lindsay was vaguely mourning the loss of her heroic King Arthur.

CHAPTER 18

Lindsay had to admit that maybe she hadn't taken this betrothal business seriously enough until she discovered how closely Giles was following her everywhere she went. Obviously, Father felt it was very important that Lindsay maintain a good name and keep away from Arthur. At any rate, she was unable to meet Arthur in the garden the next night as planned, or any night after, for that matter.

The only privacy she still had was in her room at night, and she became so desperate to get in touch with Arthur that she finally had to turn to the only person she could trust: Dorothy. Dorothy came to her room every night before she fell asleep, a ritual that was just short of tucking her in. After several days of unsuccessfully trying to dodge Giles' watchful eyes, Lindsay finally worked up the courage to speak to Dorothy.

The older woman was bustling around the room, drawing the heavy shutters against the chill autumn evening. Lin sat in her bed with the covers around her, hugging her knees. When Dorothy came over to give her a final goodnight, Lindsay chose her moment and took a deep breath.

"Dorothy I need to ask you a favor," she began, hesitantly.

Dorothy sat down beside her on the bed and patted her knee. "Of course, child," she said soothingly, "What can I help you with?"

"Well," Lindsay hedged, "You know of Arthur, who is squire to Sir Cei?" She nodded, and Lin continued more bravely. "Dorothy, I need you to deliver something to him for me."

Her face instantly registered disapproval, and Lindsay's hopes fell a little. She had been gambling on the chance that Dorothy might not have heard anything about her and Arthur. Dorothy opened her mouth to speak, but Lin rushed in first.

"Oh, please, Dorothy," she pleaded softly, clutching at her arm, "Father and Giles won't allow me near him, and it's very important that I get a message to him!"

Dorothy was frowning. "Your father has made it very clear that you are not to see or communicate with him," she said severely, "Not with your wedding being arranged. Lindsay, my lamb, he knows what is best. This Arthur, he has nothing to offer you."

"But you're so wrong!" Lin cried out, unable to stop herself, "If you only knew…Someday he'll be king."

"King? That young man?" scoffed Dorothy, "Really, Lindsay."

"I'm not making it up," she said, close to tears, "Please, Dorothy, can't you understand? I love him!"

Dorothy looked at her sorrowfully. "Love hasn't much to do with marriage," she reminded, gently, "There are other considerations, many of them. My dear, you are like a daughter to me, and I can't allow you to ruin your life over a foolish whim."

It was almost a direct echo of her father's words. "Dorothy," Lindsay tried again, looking her squarely in the eyes, "Please. Just give him this note for me. That's all. I just need to explain what's going on and why I haven't met him, and to say goodbye. Nothing more. Please…I owe him this much." Of course she was lying. Dorothy didn't need to know what was really written in the sealed note that she'd written out that afternoon: specific plans for when she and Arthur would run away together.

Dorothy seemed to be wavering a little, so Lindsay pushed one last time. "Please," she repeated quietly, "Please, Dorothy. Haven't you ever loved someone who was forbidden to you?"

Dorothy sighed, and gazed at her work-worn hands for a moment. "Yes, I have," she said, which surprised Lin, coming from this plain, no-nonsense woman. Suddenly, out of nowhere, she had a vivid recollection of the looks that had passed between Dorothy and her father when they first arrived home. Could it be?

Dorothy rose while Lin was still studying her speculatively, and held out her hand for the note.

"I'll deliver your message," she said, almost brusquely, and then left the room before Lindsay could thank her. Lin felt rather bereft after she'd gone, somehow realizing that she'd sacrificed something in her relationship with the woman who was the closest thing to a mother she had in this place. But she comforted herself by curling up under the covers and daydreaming about the life she would have with Arthur. It would be worth it, to be with him.

Dorothy came back the following night, just long enough to silently deliver a note from Arthur and then depart. In the most romantic, chivalrous language she'd ever read, Arthur told Lindsay that he had decided to agree to her plans. During the confusion and festivities of Cei and Alyce's wedding and feasting, they would slip out and ride toward London together.

The days tumbled by until it was a mere two days before the wedding. Lindsay was formally betrothed to Sir Cedric in a ceremony that seemed to be little more than signing names to a written marriage agreement. Lin let it wash over her and watched Sir Cedric, with his red hair, red beard, and redder face, thinking with amusement how angry he'd be when his intended bride disappeared. Lindsay's efforts to remain calm and above suspicion seemed to work, because Giles' surveillance lapsed a bit and Father even gave her a few smiling glances now and then.

Everyone seemed to think that she was now meek and subservient, but inside she was laughing.

She spent her last afternoon with Aunt Sam. The two of them had become distant since Garrick had returned to the castle, which actually worked out for the best since it gave Samantha fewer opportunities to become suspicious of Lindsay. That day they sat in the garden, enjoying the last of the fall sun and taking a break from the frantic wedding preparations.

"I can hardly remember what it was like, sometimes, going to high school back in New Hampshire," Lin remarked lazily, basking in the feel of the sunshine on her face. "I've gotten pretty comfortable here."

"This definitely can grow on you," Samantha agreed, "Providing you don't get sick, and have enough to eat, and aren't involved in any wars. But we mustn't forget that soon it will be time to get you home again, before your marriage can take place. Imagine what sort of reception you'd get if you returned home newly married and possibly pregnant!"

"Ugh," Lindsay shuddered, thinking of Sir Cedric's beefy red hands.

Funny how Samantha wasn't even pretending anymore that she had no control over Lindsay's coming and going. It didn't matter. Soon Lin would be beyond her reach anyway, for she doubted Aunt Sam could send her home if she didn't even know where to find her. Perhaps she'd even think that Lin had suddenly been transported home magically on her own. Lindsay didn't really care. She no longer had any real reason to want to go home, anyway.

Her comment did make Lin feel a little panicky, though. She wasn't naive, and she'd had those awful health classes in school like everyone else. Running off with Arthur was probably going to involve new aspects of their relationship that she wasn't sure she was ready to handle. And they didn't exactly have a Planned Parenthood office nearby.

Samantha suddenly sat up a little straighter and looked at her niece with narrowed eyes. Lin remembered belatedly that she needed to blank out her thoughts, and after a moment her aunt's scrutiny subsided, although she looked vaguely worried.

"I would have expected you to protest a bit more about going home," she said, oh-so-casually.

"If anything, I should be mad at you for pretending that you couldn't easily send me there," Lin responded, lightly, "And besides, what am I supposed to do? Marry Sir Cedric? I don't think so!" She was quiet for a moment, then added, "Anyway, it will be a relief, too, to go home and be myself again. It's weird…since I've been here, I can't seem to read people very well anymore. Everything's sort of muted, and people's thoughts don't take me unawares. Does that happen to you?"

"A little," Samantha admitted, "I'm stronger than you, and older, and I've always tried to exercise my telepathy instead of denying it, the way you did. I think we can just chalk it up to the strain of time travel, and maybe even say that our minds are different from those of these people, and perhaps we can't receive them as easily."

"Oh. Well, anyway…are you going to come home with me?"

"No, I don't think so," Samantha replied, "After all, everyone thinks I'm on an extended research trip, so I have all the time in the world. And I am on one, really." She chuckled, and Lin did, too, imagining the looks on the faces of all her stuffy colleagues if they could see her now, sitting here in her work gown and smudged apron, hair hidden beneath her headdress.

Lindsay did think about her parents and sisters for a moment. They probably still didn't even know that she was gone. For the first time it gave her a pang, wondering how they would react when they finally realized that neither she nor Aunt Sam were ever returning home. But surely being with Arthur would more than make up for the loss of her family and her old existence.

The sun began to sink behind the walls, and their warm, peaceful respite in the garden was ending. Samantha gathered up her neglected embroidery with a sigh, and then leaned over to give Lindsay an uncharacteristic kiss on the forehead.

"Time to resume preparations for the big day tomorrow," she said, "Sleep well tonight, Lin, and enjoy the wedding, and when the dust has settled we'll decide when to send you home. I'll almost hate to see you go, it's been so pleasant having you here with me."

Lin squeezed her hand, and sat for a moment, watching her go back into the castle. For a fleeting instant she wondered if she was really doing the right thing after all, but it passed and she resolutely turned her thoughts to the new life that lay ahead, starting tomorrow.

CHAPTER 19

From the first moment of Cei and Alyce's wedding day, when Dorothy hurriedly woke Lindsay at dawn, she was kept so busy that she could hardly spare a moment to even think about her own plans. She was needed to help with the final arrangements for the wedding feast, and she scurried around all morning until it was time for the chapel ceremony.

The actual wedding wasn't nearly as elaborate as Lindsay would have expected: no grand procession up the aisle, no attendants, and no music. Lindsay couldn't help wondering if someday soon she would be in a church like this, marrying Arthur. Lady Alyce looked anxious and pale, and Lindsay's heart went out to her despite the nature of their previous encounters. Would she have looked the same, if she had to marry Sir Cedric? At least Sir Cei was young and attractive.

The feast after the wedding made up for any previous lack of festivity. Every table in the great hall was filled, and there was plenty of drinking and loud carousing from the very start. Lin hovered in the shadows of the hallway, planning to stay only until she could safely slip away and not be missed. Then she would change her clothes and gather her few possessions together. She stepped forward into the room just far enough to catch Arthur's eye. She gave him a quick nod, and he grinned in return. The signal was given and they would meet at the gate in an hour's time. Then Lindsay turned and slipped out of the hall and up the stairs to her room. She never noticed that the Lady Mary had followed all her movements with great interest.

The room upstairs was quiet after the din of the revelry below, which made her ears ring slightly. Lindsay gathered together a few of her gowns, and took off the ornate tunic she had worn for the wedding, replacing it with one less conspicuous. Then she went to the mirror to braid her hair and cover it with a face-concealing veil.

Lindsay leaned her elbows on the tall chest and studied her face closely. It was the same girl, the same Lindsay Hopkins she'd been seeing in the mirror all her life, but she felt oddly detached from the face that she saw reflected there. She was still fifteen, but she felt so much older. A month ago she had been an awkward high school sophomore who had never been on a date or even had a serious conversation with a boy, let alone running away with one. And yet it didn't all show in her face, as she might have expected. She felt so different inside, so why was she the same on the outside?

"Well, well, well," a voice said suddenly, from behind Lindsay, "Admiring yourself for your lover?"

Lindsay whirled around and there was Lady Mary, standing in the doorway with her usual unattractive sneer.

"Hello, Mary," she said coolly, fighting to stay calm, "What brings you away from the festivities?"

Mary sauntered into the room, sniffing visibly at the lack of luxury. "Oh, I was curious as to just what you might be up to." she said, gingerly seating herself on the bed after prowling around the entire room.

"I needed to freshen up a little," Lindsay replied, beginning to feel nervous. Mary didn't appear to be going anywhere any too soon, and the hour was fast running out.

"How odd," Mary remarked. 'I know you peasants like to be comfortable, but I doubt that your father would countenance an outfit like that at a wedding feast. Maybe you were thinking of, oh, perhaps going somewhere?"

Lindsay's head snapped around. Mary was fanning herself with a folded piece of paper that looked suspiciously like her note to Arthur.

"Seems that you warn that lover of yours to be a bit less careless with his personal correspondence," Mary drawled, in response to the unasked question, "Very irresponsible of him, leaving this lying about."

Lindsay felt her face flush with anger, and she lunged for the note. Mary just laughed nastily, and being taller, simply stood up and waved it tantalizingly out of reach until Lindsay gave up, disheveled and furious.

"All right," she said, "Tell me what you want."

Mary's eyes narrowed and glinted dangerously. "Want? Why Lindsay, I don't want anything from you. I just want to enjoy the look on your face before I go down and fetch your father, or perhaps that watchdog big brother of yours. He'd be very interested in this, I'm sure."

"But why?" Lindsay cried, hopelessly, "Why do this? If I leave with Arthur, then Sir Cedric will be all yours again. It will work out for both of us!"

"Liar!" she hissed. "He won't ever come back to me. I'm not a suitable marriage prospect anymore. He'll just find someone else with a good-sized dowry. No, Lady Lindsay, this is purely for revenge. Revenge for stealing him, for ranking yourself up with the rest of us, and for all those times at school when you acted too good for us."

Her face was contorted and Lindsay was frightened of her, but also desperate. "Please, Mary," she pleaded wildly, "Please. You don't know what this means to me."

Mary just gave Lindsay a triumphant smile, and straightened her skirts with exaggerated care. "Oh, you're wrong there." she said, practically purring, "I know exactly what this means to you. And that's why I'm going to enjoy it so much." With that, she left the room, and Lindsay could hear her unhurried steps descending the stairs.

Lindsay panicked. How much time did she have before Father or Dorothy or Samantha appeared? She threw on her cloak and picked up her bundle, casting one last look around the room before hurrying down the stairs. If she could just get to the hallway and sneak out through the kitchens…She crept stealthily down the last few steps, peering cautiously around before dashing for the kitchen door.

"Are you leaving us, Lindsay?" a familiar voice said quietly, above the noise of the great hall, and Lin closed her eyes in despair. When she opened them again, there stood Dorothy and Samantha, Dorothy with a sorrowful expression on her kind face, and Aunt Sam's eyes bright with anger. Mary stood behind them, making no attempt to conceal her malicious smile. Beyond her, the revelry continued unabated, as more toasts were raised to the bride and groom.

Aunt Sam took Lindsay firmly by the elbow, Dorothy removed the bundle from her unresisting grasp, and between them they steered her back up the stairs. Lindsay let them lead her, numbly wondering just how long Arthur would wait in the chilling air before he decided that she had changed her mind.

The two women took her back into her bedroom. Dorothy unfastened her cloak, clucking gently, "Oh, Lindsay, child," in a distressed murmur, "If I had known what was really in the message…"

Aunt Sam looked at her sharply, from where she was leaning against the wall, contemplating Lindsay. "Message?" she inquired, with a dangerous edge to her voice.

"A note," Lindsay said dully, "Dorothy delivered it to Arthur after Father forbid me to speak to him."

"I didn't realize what she had written," Dorothy said sadly, "She misled me. Otherwise I never would have delivered it." She seemed somewhat cowed by Samantha's overly bright gaze.

"We shall discuss it later," Samantha said, dismissively, "Dorothy, if you would leave us, please?" Dorothy nodded and crept away, and Lindsay came out of her misery a little by the unexpectedly steely note of command in her aunt's voice. She had never before thought of Dorothy as a servant to them.

Lindsay waited until Dorothy's footsteps had been swallowed up by the noise below, and then turned to face Samantha. "Well, now what?" she said, flatly, "You've wrecked my life. What else?"

Samantha studied her keenly. "Wrecked **your** life, have I?" she said, sharply, "Lindsay, you almost succeeded in destroying Arthur's entire future and his legacy to generations to come!"

"You can't know that for sure," Lindsay replied, through gritted teeth. "Together he and I could have surpassed the legends. There would never be a Guinever to betray him. I could have made things work out right."

Aunt Sam laughed tiredly. "You don't get it, do you, Lindsay? Part of the importance of the legend lies in the betrayal. And if he ran off with you, Arthur might very well never have become king at all. No sword in the stone, no round table…Nothing."

"Well, as my mother would say, it's all academic now," Lindsay replied bitterly, sitting down o the bed and removing the hot veil from her hair. "What now? Slap my hands and send me to bed? Marry me off to Cedric?"

"I should think you could figure it out," Samantha said calmly, "I shall have to send you home now, of course. I can't trust you anymore."

"No!" Lindsay shrieked, suddenly jumping up and rushing for the door, "No! You can't send me home! Not now!"

'I have to," she said, almost to herself, as she easily caught Lindsay in a tight embrace. Lin struggled futilely, then gave up, and buried her face in her aunt's neck, sobbing bitterly.

"Lindsay," she murmured, "To protect you, and Arthur…I have no choice."

"No…" Lin cried desperately, but then her mind was filled with the image of the Malory book that Aunt Sam had sent to her, so long ago it seemed now. She saw the faces of her parents and sisters, her home, her room. She felt Aunt Sam stroking her hair and whispering in her ear, "Yes, think about the book, and about your family…" and Lindsay knew that the images were coming into her mind from her aunt's. And then things grew fuzzy inside her head, and when she finally opened her eyes again Aunt Sam was gone and Lindsay was once again sitting on the high school stage, stiff and cramped, and Chris was shaking her and saying her name. The Malory book had fallen to the floor, lying bereft, its binding broken.

CHAPTER 20

"Lindsay! C,mon, Lin, wake up!"

Lindsay opened her eyes reluctantly, blinking as she tried to clear her blurry vision. Chris was shaking her shoulder almost viciously and hissing her name as people streamed back into the auditorium to resume rehearsal. Lin looked up at Chris in confusion, unable to make the transition back to the present, and Chris finally kicked her none too gently in the leg.

"Come on, Lindsay," she hissed again, even more vehemently, "Everyone's coming back from dinner and you look like an absolute jerk, asleep in the middle of the stage. Do you want them to laugh at you?"

Goaded by Chris, Lindsay finally staggered groggily to her feet and stumbled off the stage into the wings, where she could stop and lean against the prop room door. A wave of despair swept over her as she began to realize that she really was back in her own time again. Everything around her looked foreign, as if she were watching it all in a movie, and her mind was having difficulty adjusting to what she was seeing. Kids in ripped up jeans, kids with strange haircuts, girls in mini skirts or leggings, laughing and talking and making out in the corners. Lindsay felt oddly naked in her own jeans, after the accustomed weight of a long, heavy skirt. All the long-familiar surroundings were now strange, so how could so little time have passed for her here?

Chris came around the curtain, looking a little anxious and carrying the Malory book, now in rather sorry condition.

"Are you all right, Lin?" she asked, with more sympathy than she had shown a few minutes before. "You seemed so...strange out there, when I woke you up. Do you feel okay?"

She did look genuinely concerned, so Lindsay made an effort to compose herself. "I'm better now, Chris," she said slowly, "I guess I was really tired. Maybe I'm getting sick or something." She took the book from Chris, grabbing at a few of the pages as they drifted loose from the broken binding. Chris continued to look at her skeptically, and her gaze was unnerving and irritating.

"I'm fine, Chris!" Lindsay repeated, a little more strongly than she'd intended, "Just leave me alone!"

Chris' face darkened. "Well excuse me!" she snapped, and flounced back through the curtain, but Lindsay was too tired and confused and stricken to care. She heard Mrs. Cummings start the rehearsal again, and the piano began plinking out a song. Lindsay slid down against the door until she was sitting on the floor, still fighting the terrible feeling of disorientation. She leaned her head back as the curtain open, watching the still-clumsy cast attempting some sort of choreography. It was supposed to be a scene of formal dancing at King Arthur's court, and it was such a cheap and lifeless version of the dancing that had taken place at Cei and Alyce's wedding feast that Lin's eyes began to swim.

She couldn't believe that Aunt Sam had sent her back like that, instantly, without a chance to say any good-byes, or even explain things to Arthur. Perhaps Lin had even hoped that she could somehow prevent her aunt from sending her home at all, especially if she'd been far off with Arthur. But Samantha had proven that she was much stronger, and had shunted Lindsay home like a recalcitrant child. Lindsay's heart ached to be with Arthur again, to be riding off to London on their way to a new life together, just as they'd planned. She didn't want to be back here, in this colorless modern life where no one especially cared for her and life was endlessly boring and frustrating. The rest of her life seemed to stretch out before her as a procession of gray, monotonous years. Lindsay put her head down on her knees and began to cry in earnest.

A little while later she felt a hand on her shoulder. Her sister Kathi was crouched down beside her. Lindsay's spirits lifted slightly because it was wonderful to see her face again. She wanted to throw her arms around Kathi, and restrained herself only because she knew Kathi would really think something major was wrong.

"Lin, are you okay?" Kathi asked softly, "Chris came and told me that you were crying."

Lindsay thought, a little nastily, that no one here seemed to be capable of progressing beyond the word "okay", but she snuffled a bit and swiped at her eyes.

"I don't feel too great, Kath," she said, in a low voice, finding that she had to make an effort to speak in the high school lingo, without any of the expressions that her tongue wanted to use after her time in the castle. "It must be the flu or something."

"I'll take you home, then," Kathi said, her face filled with concern, "Just let me tell Mrs. Cummings. Good thing Mom let me have the car." She hurried off, and Lindsay struggled to her feet again and collected her coat and books, which is no small accomplishment when you haven't seen them in a month. Kathi solicitously helped her to the car, and soon they were headed home. Lindsay was still looking around her with the eyes of a stranger, trying to reacquaint herself with the twenty-first century and growing more and more exhausted.

Walking back into the brightly-lit kitchen at home was like a dream, and her parents' faces had never been so dear to her. It was odd, too, sort of like those homecomings from summer camp when you felt like you had grown and changed incredibly, and yet once you were home nothing was different and no one seemed to notice any change in you. But Lindsay had forgotten just how much her family and this house meant to her, and she went straight into her mother's arms as if she were five years old and not fifteen. She was so tired and drained, and just wanted to be taken care of.

Her mom tucked her into bed like a little girl and Lindsay fell asleep to the familiar sounds of the household around her. For a while she forgot all about her longing for Arthur and the castle and just snuggled under the covers, warm and safe and glad to be home.

CHAPTER 21

It was surprisingly easy to fall back into a routine. Lindsay spent a few more days pretending to have the flu, which gave her some time to get over the shock of being so rudely returned to her own time. After that it was easier to resume the pattern of school and play rehearsals and home life with every appearance of normality. Inside her head, however, it wasn't so easy: she was still going around in a fog, seeing the world around her but not really feeling like a part of it. It was like reading a wonderful book, one that gets you so caught up in the story that once it's finished you can't tear yourself away from the mood and characters because you still feel so involved with them. The story has become your own life, to the point where the everyday world seems dull and a little unreal. Lindsay still felt like she belonged in Arthur's world and was just a spectator in her own, participating in her usual activities but feeling distanced.

"Camelot" was due to open in just three weeks, and Mrs. Cummings imposed a frantic pace on everyone that did a lot toward keeping Lindsay occupied and from dwelling too much on Arthur and the life she was missing at the castle. Lindsay still went through her days wondering what was going on there: if Arthur had now returned home with Cei and Alyce, if Garrick was still with Samantha, and what it was like to spend the winter in a castle. And there was the nagging knowledge that time was passing in Arthur's world much more quickly than it was for

Lindsay. For all she knew, days were passing there every time she wasted minutes in Algebra and phys-ed.

The Malory book sat on her desk at home. She had not tried to read it again, knowing instinctively that it had only been an accessory to time travel and wouldn't be able to return her to Arthur just by itself. Lindsay knew that her entrance into that world had been wholly due to Aunt Sam. The only chance she had to ever get back would be to somehow spend time with Aunt Sam and try to worm it out of her, either through telepathy or just in casual conversation. After all, if their talents were so alike, shouldn't Lindsay be able to learn how to time-travel on her own? But she didn't even know if Aunt Sam had returned to the present day yet, so most of Lindsay's hopes were pretty dim.

Or so she thought. It was the Monday before "Camelot" was to open, and Lindsay and Kathi were just dragging themselves home from a long and tiring rehearsal. Mrs. Cummings was feeling the pressure and was pushing everyone, and Lindsay felt particularly numb and exhausted. She was still finding it difficult to adjust to the frantic pace of her modern life after the slower days of the castle. She stumbled off the bus after her sister, shivering a little in the chill November dusk and looking forward to the warm, fragrant kitchen.

"Hi, Mom," Kathi called out, as they both dumped their neglected homework on the table.

"Girls!" Mom greeted them, bustling in from the study, "I thought you'd never get home…I have some wonderful news!" Kathi shot Lindsay an amused glance. Their mom did seem like a little kid about to burst with a secret.

"Your aunt just called!" she continued, and Lindsay suddenly pricked up her ears, from where she had slumped in the big easy chair by the fireplace. They only had one aunt, and if she was calling, that meant she was home…

"She's long overdue for a visit," Mom was saying happily, "And since both of you are involved in the play, Samantha has decided to fly in on

Wednesday to see the show and spend a few weeks!"

Both girls shrieked appreciatively, since it had been such a long time (at least for Kathi) since they'd seen her. Inwardly Lindsay rejoiced even more. Circumstances couldn't be more perfect, and if she could work things out as she wanted to, she might even be with Arthur again within a week. Even the thought of it seemed to bring her back to life from deep inside, although she certainly wasn't naive enough to ignore all the difficulties. First of all, Aunt Sam would do everything in her power to prevent Lindsay from returning to Arthur, if she ever had the slightest inkling of Lin attempting to do so. Lindsay would bet anything that this visit of hers was largely intended to check up on her, and not just from some burning desire to see her New England relatives again. Lindsay would have to be very careful and very wily. This time she would not be afraid to use every ounce of power she had in order to read her aunt's thoughts. Samantha was the only chance for returning to Arthur.

Lindsay gazed into the flickering flames of the fire as her mother and sister chatted excitedly. Where was Arthur now, and how would she find him when she returned to his time? Lindsay had no idea how old Arthur had been when he was crowned king. What if he was already king by the time she returned? She'd have to read some of the legends and try to find out where he spent his time. Perhaps the castle gossips would know. It was going to be a challenge. All in all, it seemed that Lindsay had a lot to do before her aunt arrived.

Mom picked up Aunt Sam at the airport on Wednesday afternoon, and she was sitting in the kitchen when Kathi and Lindsay arrived home from a dress rehearsal. Lindsay found it was rather a shock to see her aunt in modern clothing. She also noticed how very pale and tired Samantha looked, more than you'd be just from jet lag. Lindsay made sure that her greeting was just as enthusiastic as Kathi's. They had a long and noisy family dinner, with everyone talking at once. Lindsay smirked inwardly as Samantha smoothly told stories of her supposed research trips all over Europe.

"I've been doing some fascinating research on the Arthurian legends," Aunt Sam was saying, in response to a question Lindsay's father had asked. She slowly sipped her coffee. "Scholars have been trying for years to determine whether or not Arthur actually existed in history, and I've been chasing down ancient historical sources and scurrying around the archeological sites. It's been quite wonderful, really."

Why don't you tell them how wonderful Garrick is, too? Lindsay thought to herself.

Shut up, Lindsay, her aunt's amused voice said inside Lin's mind. Lin looked up at her, startled, then grinned. Then she started to imagine Aunt Sam running around the castle with a pick and shovel and cameras, instead of the big ring of keys that Lindsay had become accustomed to seeing her wield as she swept through the kitchens and storerooms, commanding and admonishing servants, and running the household.

"I always thought it was accepted that King Arthur was just a myth," Lindsay's father remarked.

Aunt Sam looked thoughtful. "It was considered to be just a legend for many years," she admitted, "But there are too many enticing little clues to just ignore. He may not have existed as a king, but possibly as some sort of warrior or chieftan."

Lindsay wanted to giggle again. She had a sudden vivid image of Arthur clothed as some sort of Indian chief of the old west, ridiculously enough, and it certainly didn't fit well with her memory of him. She sternly admonished herself to be careful. Every word Aunt Sam spoke seemed to make her more giddy, like a little kid who belonged to a secret club and could hardly keep it secret. If she continued like this, her aunt would grow suspicious of her behavior and she would never find out how to return to Arthur. She already knew that Aunt Sam was monitoring her thoughts.

"It certainly would've been neat to have known the real Arthur," Kathi remarked innocently. Lindsay felt the color rush to her cheeks and she kept her eyes on her plate.

Everyone laughed at that, leading into an animated conversation about characters in history they would most like to meet.

"I agree with Kathi," her mother said, "It would be fascinating to spend an evening with Arthur. Imagine what he could tell us!"

"On second thought, maybe I'd prefer someone less ancient," Kathi said, with a frown, "Someone more recent. Then there wouldn't be such a culture gap. Can you imagine trying to explain computers and fax machines and cars to someone from the dark ages?"

"That would be the problem, you see," Aunt Sam said, seriously, "We can't even begin to imagine the consequences of altering history. It would be almost impossible to keep from telling everyone about all the wonders that the future holds. It would give you such power. So say we tell Arthur, for instance, that his wife Guinever will betray him and his Round Table will fall. So what if he then decides not to marry, or never to become anything other than the usual petty, warring chieftain? Britain is never united under his rule, and his ideals of government are never realized, however briefly. Who knows? The end result could be our living under a dictatorship instead of a democracy."

Kathi looked somewhat overwhelmed, but Lindsay's face was flaming again. She knew that entire little lecture had been for her benefit, and it made her angry. Being careful to look Aunt Sam straight in the face, she said, "I think it could just as easily work out for the best. There are plenty of situations in history that could benefit from a little timely intervention. Let's say that Arthur refuses to marry Guinever. So he takes another wife, one who gives him a son, thus preventing his kingdom from ever falling into the hands of Mordred, his illegitimate son. Camelot doesn't fall, and generations of Arthurian kings bring lasting peace to England."

Lindsay subsided, feeling triumphant, as her family looked at her quizzically.

"You've certainly picked up a lot of history, doing this show," Lin's father remarked, impressed.

But Aunt Sam shook her head ruefully. "It sounds very nice, Lindsay, but you still don't know what else might happen because you tampered with the way things were supposed to be."

"Goodness!" Lindsay's mother exclaimed, "You'd think that the two of you were ready to step into a time machine tomorrow. However, it's getting late and you must be exhausted, Sam."

"Yes, the jet lag is setting in," Samantha admitted, with a yawn, "Time to get to bed before I collapse. Lin, would you help me with my things?"

"Sure," Lindsay replied, through her teeth, still irritated with her aunt. After the usual round of kisses and goodnights, Lin led her aunt upstairs to the big guestroom at the back of the house. She dumped the incredibly heavy suitcase on the luggage rack and then flopped down on her aunt's bed. Samantha took off her skirt and sweater and put on a fuzzy old bathrobe, then curled herself into the big upholstered armchair in the corner.

She looked at Lindsay with a somewhat grim expression, then said, "All right, Lindsay. Let's have it out."

CHAPTER 22

Lindsay pulled herself into a sitting position on the bed, crossing her legs and resting her face on her hands. She was trying to decide on the best way to approach this whole business, calculating how to get the most information out of her aunt without arousing too much suspicion.

"I'm already suspicious, Lindsay," her aunt said smoothly, and Lin groaned.

"Why do I keep forgetting how easily you can do that?" she complained. "All right, Aunt Sam. I won't sneak around. I want to know the truth about how you brought me to the castle and then sent me home again. How did you get to the castle in the first place? I know you had more to do with it than you let on."

Aunt Sam sighed wearily, running a pale hand through her hair, and Lindsay was again struck by how worn and thin she looked.

"I guess it is time to tell you the whole story," Samantha admitted, "You're safe at home now, so I suppose I can tell you the truth." She spoke reluctantly, though, as she continued. "I will, however, take the liberty of editing where necessary, in case you consider yourself capable of running back to Camelot the moment my back is turned."

Lindsay blushed, wondering just how transparent she was, but then she thought that there was hope, if Aunt Sam even faintly assumed that Lin might be capable of the time travel by herself.

"Well," Aunt Sam said, pulling her robe more tightly around her,"It all started with the research I was doing, about the authenticity of the Arthur legends. I was spending much of my time buried in old books and manuscripts and really becoming involved with the stories and characters. It was almost beginning to feel as if their world was more real to me than my own."

Lindsay nodded, knowing exactly what she meant.

"In all this research I first ran across a mention of Sir Garrick. He was intriguing, not flamboyant like Arthur or his famous knights. Arthur was too legendary for my tastes, but Garrick appealed to me, from accounts given of him and from his own writings."

"So you fell in love with him," Lindsay stated, rather triumphantly, still smarting from her remark about Arthur being "flamboyant".

Aunt Sam smiled, and its warmth reached her eyes, changing her whole face the same way as when Garrick returned to the castle.

"Yes, I have to admit to that," she said, with a soft laugh, "I fell in love with a knight who had lived hundreds of years before me, if indeed he had ever existed at all, which I couldn't absolutely prove. And then, in the library of a private manor house, where I had permission to do research, I found an original manuscript of Garrick's writings. Finding the book was what brought me to Garrick, although in a slightly different manner from what I originally told you." She grinned maddeningly, knowing full well that she was withholding the most tantalizing piece of information.

Lindsay was furious, but calm. With enormous effort, she pasted a bland little smile on her own face, and then concentrated on her aunt's thoughts with more strength than she had ever dared to use before. Maybe Samantha's defenses were weakened, since she was obviously tired and vulnerable, but for the first time the habitual thought-concealing blackness lifted, just for a moment. Lindsay could catch a few disconnected images: her aunt, holding Garrick's book lovingly in her hands, concentrating all her abilities on her knowledge of the world and the man who had created those pages. No magic charms, no secret spells, just the power of her mind and the fact that she was trying to enter a world that had already become quite real to her. Why couldn't Lindsay do it, too? Was her longing for Arthur's world strong enough to carry her there, even with mental powers that were less than Samantha's?

Lindsay was so excited that she had to make a conscious effort to keep her expression neutral and her thoughts shielded. Aunt Sam continued the conversation.

"Yes, the book was actually Sir Garrick's own writings," she was saying, dreamily, "An original, in his own handwriting, can you believe it? Of inestimable value, lying about in a private library unprotected. The owners obviously had no idea of its value or else they would have sold it off years ago to pay their debts! And yet it was even more valuable to me, because eventually it took me to Garrick himself. They were happy with the several hundred pounds...about $400...that I gave them for it."

The book. An object saturated with a strong sense of its time and place. The pieces of the puzzle were falling into place bit by bit, the puzzle of how Samantha went to Garrick.

"So you went back in time to find some man you'd fallen in love with through some old books," Lindsay said incredulously. "This sounds like the conversation we just had at dinner. In your own way, you're as bad as I am!"

"I don't think so!" her aunt replied, fiercely, anger sparking her eyes as she rose and paced the room. "First of all, Garrick has none of the historical significance of Arthur. I already knew that he had lived a comparatively unremarked life, which my presence wouldn't alter that much. Secondly, the opportunity to observe Arthur and his era firsthand, and to validate all the legends about him, was one that I couldn't resist. What scholar could? So I went."

"And all this time I was supposed to be under the impression that this time travel business was some sort of cosmic coincidence," Lindsay said bitterly, "Something that just happens to you out of the blue. Shazam, the magic book genie whisks you back in time and then whisks you home again. But it's actually a deliberate process, and all along you knew exactly how to go and come back again. You were never really worried that I might have to marry Sir Cedric. I feel like the mouse after the cat's been playing with it."

"That's not true, Lindsay," Aunt Sam protested quietly, sinking into her chair again, "Bringing you to the castle was an accident. I sent you the Malory book without realizing what a strong talisman it was, permeated with all my childish longings to visit the time of Arthur. Somehow, coupled with your dissatisfaction with your life here, and the atmosphere of Camelot surrounding you from the play, you ended up there, too. I wasn't at all sure that I would be able to successfully send you home the same way I'd come home myself. My initial arrival at the castle was a combination of luck and chance. I've always been intrigued by time travel, but I never thought I'd actually be able to make it work. It was the intensity of my longing for Garrick, and my loneliness, and a mind which is more powerful than most. Believe me, Lindsay, you can't imagine how shocked I was when you suddenly arrived at the castle. I felt responsible, yet powerless."

Lindsay's heart went out to her, despite the feeling that she had been tricked somehow. She had never imagined that Aunt Sam was anything other than happy and independent, but it occurred to her now that Samantha had led a lonely life for years, with no mention of boyfriends.

"Well, I guess I can see how it happened," Lindsay finally remarked, grudgingly, "Anyway, what now?"

"Nothing now." her aunt replied firmly. "This is too dangerous and unknown to fool with. There is no guarantee for either of us to be able to get in or out again, and this increases the possibility of getting trapped in time. Perhaps it would be tolerable for me, but not for you, to give up your future here. Besides, Arthur is coming into his own now. I will not allow you to jeopardize his destiny."

"One more question, then," Lindsay said, deciding not to get into another argument about altering history. "Were you able to discover, after you sent me home, if there was another 'real' Lindsay to take my place?"

"Now that was interesting," her aunt replied, perking up a bit, "I was also curious about that, but as soon as you left it was as if you had never been there at all. I was the only one who seemed to remember you. Nobody mentioned your name, so I am assuming that you and I created our own places in the family when we were present, complete with our past histories. Once we left, there were no traces of us anymore. It's a little eerie, especially thinking that my husband is only married to me when I'm actually there!"

Lindsay shivered a little. It was sort of a chilling idea, and she wasn't too thrilled to realize that Arthur wouldn't be pining for her now and had, in fact, forgotten her existence. But at least there wasn't another Lindsay running amuck there, getting herself married to Sir Cedric and lousing things up.

"So, my sweet," Aunt Sam said, with a huge yawn, "Just be thankful that you had the experience of being there and were lucky enough to really know Arthur, however briefly. I think I shall always envy you your relationship with him, even if I would never have dared." She yawned again. "And now I'm going to kick you out because I'm falling asleep."

"Yes," Lindsay replied absently, because something she had said earlier was nagging at Lin. "You look terrible, you should get some rest." Lindsay didn't notice the look of dismay that crossed Samantha's face, because she suddenly realized just what it was that had been bothering her.

"Camelot." Lindsay said it flatly, and Samantha looked at her quizzically. "You said you didn't want me to go running back to Camelot, and yet Camelot wasn't even built until Arthur was already king." A sudden fear clutched at her. "Oh, Aunt Sam, has so much time passed there? Is Arthur king now, so soon?"

Her aunt gazed at her sympathetically. "He will be crowned king in London, in a few days' time there," she said gently, "He has plans for the construction of Camelot to begin next summer, in his time."

Lindsay swallowed hard. "And Guinever?"

Samantha must have felt some pity for her, since after all their situations weren't so different. As far as she was concerned, Lin was safely within her own time again and would never be able to return to Arthur's side. So she was offering some small comfort when she said, "Arthur won't marry Guinever for the better part of a year or so yet."

Lindsay closed her eyes briefly, with an inward sigh of relief, then opened them again and smiled tiredly at her aunt.

"Thank you," she said. "At least I can think of him for a little while longer, not ensnared by her yet."

Aunt Sam shook her head, but with a smile and Lindsay kissed her on the cheek before slipping out into the hallway. She closed the door behind her and leaned against it for a moment, her head spinning.

Arthur was almost king, but not yet married. Lindsay had some precious time left to get him back and marry him before Guinever became his wife. And thanks to her aunt, she now had the key to returning.

Lin hurried back to her room and locked the door. Ignoring the decrepit Malory book still on her desk, she went over to her dresser and rummaged around through the top drawer until her hand closed on the object she was searching for. Sitting on her bed, she slowly opened her fist and gazed at what was there.

It was the emerald necklace that she had worn all during her stay at the castle. For some reason it had stayed with her when she was sent back through time, safely hidden under her clothing. Lindsay turned it this way and that, watching it flash green fire and feeling excitement welling up in her again. The necklace would be the talisman necessary to help take her back to Arthur's time. Not only would she need the abilities that she shared with her aunt, but also an object to fasten on to, something that belonged wholly to the time and place she wanted to return to. Aunt Sam had traveled with the aid of Garrick's writings, and Lindsay had been sent there inadvertently because of the Malory book. Now she would use the birthstone necklace, which rightfully belonged only to the Lindsay she had been at the castle, to take herself back to Arthur.

CHAPTER 23

Now all that was left was for Lindsay to find the right time to leave. She couldn't afford to wait until Aunt Sam had gone home to England, at the rate that time was passing back in the castle world. But she knew that the amount of concentration that was going to be required for time travel would bring Aunt Sam running to her in a minute, since Lindsay wouldn't have any energy to spare for shielding her thoughts. She needed to choose a time and place where Aunt Sam couldn't get to her and stop her, once she knew what Lindsay was up to.

School was the obvious choice, and better yet, during the last performance of "Camelot". There would be a lot of confusion, Aunt Sam would be absorbed in watching the show, and if Lindsay was backstage or in the prop room, no one could get to her easily or quickly. Lindsay also had to confess that she wanted to see the show through, since it had indirectly brought her to the castle in the first place. And she didn't want to let Mrs. Cummings or her new techie friends down, either. With the cast party after the show, her parents wouldn't expect her home until late. It looked like all the details were settled.

Lindsay went through her last days at home with a mixture of anticipation and surprisingly acute homesickness. It finally dawned on her that if her plan worked, she would never see her parents or sisters or her familiar surroundings again, ever. She tried to memorize their faces and be as loving as she possibly could without arousing suspicion. And she had to constantly shield her thoughts from Aunt Sam. All in all, it was an exhausting couple of days and she was relieved when the last day finally arrived.

"Lindsay? Time to go…Mom's giving us the car," Kathi hollered up the stairs, after a quick and early supper. The cast call was for 6:00, to get into costumes and makeup and do the final checks before the show.

"Coming!" Lin yelled back, then she took one last look around her room, where she'd spent so many of the hours of her life. The emerald necklace was safely fastened around her neck, under her shirt. For a moment Lindsay toyed with the idea of leaving a note, but the whole situation was too difficult to explain and no one would probably believe her anyway. Unfortunately, they'd probably end up putting her face on a milk carton.

On impulse, Lin suddenly snatched up the color photo of her family that stood on her dresser. Quickly pulling it from the frame, she slipped it into her shirt pocket.

"Lindsay! We're gonna be late!"

"I'm coming!" Lin hurried down the stairs, kissed her parents and aunt goodbye, and joined Kathi in the car.

Everyone was keyed up with final night excitement and plans for the cast party. Lindsay did a final check of the props, then went out to say hello (and a final goodbye) to her parents. She was glad to see that they were all seated in the middle of a row, near the center of the auditorium, where it wouldn't be easy to move once the show had begun.

"Hi, honey," her mom greeted her cheerfully, "All set to go?"

Lindsay shrugged. "I suppose so. I think we're all a little tired by now. I'm glad it's the last night."

Mom exchanged one of her meaningful glances with Dad, while Aunt Sam watched bemusedly. Dad cleared his throat awkwardly.

"Lindsay," he said, keeping his voice low, "Your mother and I just wanted to let you know how proud we are of you. You got involved with the show when you really didn't want to, and you've done a terrific job."

Embarrassingly, Lindsay's eyes suddenly filled with tears. "Thanks," she said, huskily, "I'm glad I did it." She gave each of them a kiss, and Aunt Sam, too, for good measure. They wouldn't know until much later that she was really saying goodbye. For a brief moment, Lin was tempted to forget all about returning to Arthur, and just being content with her memories.

Suddenly Lindsay realized that Aunt Sam was studying her intently, with narrowed eyes, so she quickly tried to clear her mind and then hurried backstage.

Being a part of the production was fun, it really was, and Lin was glad that Mrs. Cummings had pushed her into participating. It seemed like a very long time ago, almost in another lifetime. Lin didn't feel like the same girl anymore, so awkward and withdrawn. Kathi was beautiful in her costumes and played the part of Guinever wonderfully. Lindsay found even the musical theatre version of Guinever to be distasteful, knowing that she still had to beat her in the race for Arthur. Chris also did well in her role, and Lindsay took a moment to congratulate her stiffly. Things hadn't recovered between them since that night when Lindsay had returned and treated Chris so rudely. Lin doubted that they would ever recover, if she were to stay. Chris seemed so shrill and artificial now.

The frantic scene changes and big musical numbers took place without mishap, the actors danced without tripping over each other too drastically, and it was almost time for the last scenes. Lindsay really felt like a part of the team, for the first time since she'd entered high school, and it gave her a pang. Would she miss this, when she spent her days quietly doing needlework in a solar with her ladies-in-waiting? Still, Arthur's face rose before her eyes, and his startling smile seemed to beckon her.

Lindsay set the props for the final scene, then she retreated to the dusty depths of the prop room. She pulled the family photograph from her pocket and clutched it in one hand, while clutching the emerald necklace in the other. She took one last look at the faces of her family, then closed her eyes. She tried to relax and fill her mind with images of the castle and her room there, where she had first worn the emerald necklace.

Lindsay concentrated as hard as she could. She remembered the room in as much detail as she could, looking at herself in the mirror as Dorothy fastened the emerald around her neck, the sun streaming in the window and a breeze ruffling the tapestries on the walls. She thought about Dorothy's kind, loving face, and then Arthur's, and retraced the events of their first meeting. And yet nothing was happening. Lindsay could still feel the rough cinderblock wall against her back, and hear the muted strains of the final song of the show. Frustrated, she knew that her opportunity to leave was fast running out, and soon Aunt Sam would come running backstage to find her. And she'd never have another chance.

Lindsay shut her eyes tightly and concentrated again, and for the first time in her life she put to use every ounce of mental power that she possessed. She pushed her mind as hard as she could, without any holding back, something that she had always been afraid to do before. Her longing for Arthur became so strong, as she heard the actor singing his plaintive final song onstage, that she no longer cared about anything else. Lindsay loved Arthur, purely and simply, and she wanted to be with him above all else. She forced her entire concentration upon the castle, and literally pulled herself there with her mind.

Two things happened. She had a fleeting image of Aunt Sam frantically scrambling out of her seat, panicked, trying to get to Lindsay. But then Lin felt a bolt of pain through both temples, so strong that her brain felt like it was splitting in two. She wanted to scream, but her voice was frozen, and just before she blacked out from the tearing agony in her head the sounds of the high school drama production turned into a roaring, shrieking maelstrom of sound. Unconsciousness was such a relief that Lindsay never felt the change as the rough cinderblocks became the softness of a featherbed beneath her.

CHAPTER 24

Lindsay opened her eyes slowly. The incredible brightness of the sunshine aggravated her aching head, and something seemed to be wrong with her brain. The space inside her head, which used to be filled with the vibration and echo of other people's thoughts, was now dead and flat. It was sort of like the difference between an empty, echoing room and one that was muffled by furniture and carpeting. Even when she had been at the castle, Lindsay had never felt such a lack of sensitivity.

Groaning a little, Lindsay struggled to sit up. Big mistake: the throbbing in her head grew worse and her vision blurred. What terrible thing had she done to herself, trying to get back to Arthur?

Arthur? Then it dawned on her. She was staring absently at a familiar tapestried wall as she held her fingers to her temples. She was in her room at the castle! She had done it, and she was back.

Lindsay wanted to throw off the covers and do a victory dance on the rush-strewn floor, but her head felt so fragile that all she could do was swing her legs over the edge of the bed and cautiously stand up. The floor was icy cold beneath her feet, and even in the sunshine the air was frigid, but she was so glad to be back that she scarcely noticed.

Lin stretched carefully, and something fell to the floor. She squatted with exquisite carefulness and retrieved the emerald necklace from where it gleamed among the rushes, unscathed by its travels through time. But where was the photograph, her only remembrance of home?

Lindsay searched the rushes frantically, then stood up dizzily to sift through the bedclothes. She was nearly in tears when her hand brushed a papery corner beneath the pillow. The photograph, its fresh, Technicolor faces already looking out of place here, was suddenly the dearest object in the world to Lindsay. She hugged it to her chest for a moment before hiding it carefully in the bottom of her clothing chest.

"Lindsay?" Dorothy appeared in the doorway, and Lin stood up a bit too quickly from the chest and swayed dizzily. Dorothy was quickly beside her, easing her back into bed and clucking concernedly.

"Child, I don't think it's at all wise for you to be out of your bed," she said, fussing with the pillow beneath Lin's head. "That was quite a scare you gave us yesterday, fainting away as you did."

Lindsay shut her eyes again, in another attempt to clear away some of the fuzziness in her brain. This pain in her temples was frightening. Phrases like "brain tumor" and "aneurysm" swam through her thoughts. Too many doctor shows on television, she thought ruefully. Not that it would matter much what you called it, in this place, because no one would be able to help her.

So, with that cheerful thought in mind, Lindsay opened her eyes and smiled weakly at Dorothy. "I do still feel sort of wobbly," she confessed, "But will you stay with me for a little while? It's lonely up here." And you can fill me in on some useful bits of castle gossip, she added to herself.

Dorothy smiled back, and sat down on the edge of the bed. "For a few moments only," she said, "Let's see...Your mother and father returned from the coronation in London this morning, after the weeks of festivities. How odd, to have that young squire Arthur as our new king."

Lindsay was dying to say, "I told you so," but didn't dare, as Dorothy went on.

"Your father met with Sir Cedric in London, and the date is set for the wedding, as soon as spring is upon us."

Lindsay frowned. Was that business with Cedric still in the works? She had hoped that nearly eloping with Arthur might have scared the man off for good, but it seemed he was more tenacious than she thought. Rats.

"You know," Dorothy was saying, stroking Lindsay's hair, "I never had the chance to tell you how proud I was of you, to behave so graciously after that passing foolishness with young Arthur. Of course, we could not have known he was really our true king, King Uther Pendragon's own son, but it would not have been a proper marriage. You have been a credit to your father since then, being betrothed to Sir Cedric and making up for those silly girlish fancies."

Lindsay stared at her in poorly concealed horror. What kind of nasty trick of time travel was this that she actually betrothed to that man in her absence? Lindsay had assumed that things would continue where they'd left off once she returned, and she'd still be living in the castle, unattached. How could these things happen, especially if there was no other Lindsay playing her part when she was gone? It was a big mess. If she was to marry Sir Cedric after all, then she had no time to waste in getting back to Arthur.

"I'm glad things are settled," Lindsay said, with effort, "But tell me of the coronation. Did Father speak with Arthur personally? And were Cei and Lady Alyce there?"

"Of course he saw the king," Dorothy replied, sounding puzzled, "After all, he is to be an advisor to Arthur. And Sir Cei wouldn't have missed the coronation for all the world. Did you know that he will be Arthur's seneschal, and will be instrumental in the construction of the new castle Arthur is planning? Camelot, it is to be called. And Lady Alyce is with child, I hear."

Lindsay tried to digest all this news, her head still pounding furiously. Sir Thomas as an advisor to Arthur. Well, at least he'd always know where the king was, which could be useful. It was pretty funny to think of Cei as Arthur's seneschal, after Arthur's bitter complaints about being his squire. And Alyce was pregnant, and she was younger than Lindsay was. A little shiver went up Lin's spine.

"Will the court remain in London all winter?" Lindsay asked Dorothy, casually.

"I believe so," Dorothy replied, "Camelot will begin construction in the summer, and it will be the permanent home of the king, but until then he will live in London. And his wedding will be held there as well, come summer."

She might just as well have poured cold water over Lindsay's head. "Wedding?" she squeaked, feeling breathless with shock, "But…" But Aunt Sam had promised her a year before Arthur was even betrothed!

"Yes," Dorothy prattled on, unawares, "The Lady Guinever, from the north. Her father is an important ally. It has only just been settled. Your father has promised that you may attend the wedding in London, seeing as your health prevented you from going to the coronation."

I just bet he wants me at the wedding, Lindsay thought bitterly, so that I know Arthur is permanently unattainable. You'd think he might regret the fact that I could have been queen, his own daughter.

"Dorothy," she said suddenly, unable to stop herself, "Doesn't it ever bother Father that I might be queen now, if Arthur and I had not been stopped?"

Dorothy looked troubled. "I don't know," she said truthfully, "He has never held it against Arthur, that you two tried such a foolish stunt. Perhaps he simply prefers that his daughter be married properly in the church to an honorable man, rather than to have run off in disgrace with a future king. And remember, my girl, that if Arthur had run off with you it is likely that he would not be king now. He would never have squired for Sir Cei at the great London tournament, and so never removed the sword from the stone to be declared king." She spoke gently, but there was mild reproof in her words. Apparently the whole incident had become Lindsay's fault alone, and not Arthur's. It must be nice to be a man. And how odd, that Dorothy should have echoed Aunt Sam so closely by saying that Arthur would never have become king.

"So," Lindsay said, changing the subject with forced cheerfulness, "Father and Sir Cedric have chosen a wedding date. Are they going to tell me when, or wait until that morning?"

"I believe it will be in April," Dorothy said, choosing to ignore the sarcasm, "Near St. Stephen's Day. And then you will remain with us until King Arthur's wedding festivities, after which you and your husband will go directly to your new home."

"Wonderful," Lindsay replied. April. "Dorothy, what is today? With this headache, I seem to have forgotten…"

"January 26th, the feast of St. Margaret," Dorothy said, with a worried frown. April was too soon, Lindsay thought with despair. How could she possibly get to Arthur, prevent his betrothal to Guinever, dump Sir Cedric, get to London, and at the same time avoid arousing anyone's suspicions? If only she could get rid of this terrible pain in her head…

Dorothy rose, and tucked the bedclothes more firmly around Lindsay.

"Sleep, milady," she said softly, and left the room after closing the shutters against the sunshine. Lindsay struggled to stay awake and form some sort of plan, but it was impossible. She quickly slid into a deep sleep.

CHAPTER 25

Lindsay lost most of the next few days. Most of the time she didn't even care what century she was in: everything was centered upon the excruciating pain in her head. She was vaguely aware of Dorothy's ministrations, as well as those of some of the other women in the castle who were noted healers. In her more lucid moments, Lin was terrified of what might possibly be wrong with her.

Finally she awoke one morning to find that most of the pain was gone. The throbbing was reduced to a little ache, sort of the same as eating very cold ice cream very fast. Lindsay sat up in bed gratefully. She had wasted too much precious time lying in this stupid bed, and now she had to formulate a plan for getting to Arthur.

The big question was how to get to London. If she could just see Arthur, talk with him privately, then the rest would take care of itself. Naturally Arthur would want to marry her, and since he was the king, the problem of Sir Cedric and Lady Guinever could be easily disposed of. So all Lindsay really had to do was get to Arthur, holding court in London. If only she hadn't wasted so much time with this damn headache!

Lindsay rose gingerly from the bed, expecting the floor to spin and pitch, but everything remained normal, except for the stiffness in her joints. The mirror over the chest was a shock, as she saw her face, terribly pale with big circles under the eyes. Her mother would have taken one look at her and rushed her off to the doctor...Doctor?

It was just like a cartoon light bulb going on over her head. Suddenly Lindsay knew how she could get to London, and quickly. If she could continue to convince Dorothy and her father that she was in agony from these head pains, then she could concoct a visit to see a doctor in London. Many afternoons in the solar she'd listened to tales of marvelous cures performed by several noted doctors there, and Dorothy could easily enough find out their names from the ladies. Then Lindsay would have fake enough pain to seem in danger, and yet not so weak that she couldn't travel.

Footsteps sounded on the stairs, and Lin quickly scrambled back into bed, trying to arrange herself back into an invalid pose. Moments later Dorothy bustled in, her face puckered with worry as Lindsay gave a very artful little groan into her pillow.

"How are you today, my lamb?" she inquired cheerfully, smoothing the hair off Lindsay's forehead, "Do you feel any better?"

"A bit better," Lindsay replied, with a little quaver in her voice, "But Dorothy, there is something I must ask you."

"What is it, my pet?"

Lindsay sighed dramatically, then looked Dorothy squarely in the eyes. "You and I both know that I'm not getting any better." she said simply, "And I'm afraid. I don't want to die."

Dorothy's eyes widened in sudden alarm, and she started to fuss with the bedclothes in order to conceal her face.

"Now dearest," she said soothingly, "No one is talking about dying." But Lindsay had seen that momentary panic in her expression.

Softly Lindsay continued. "We both know that something is very wrong with me," she said, trying to hold Dorothy's eyes, "And I've been remembering something that Lady Marie was telling us one day, about that doctor she took her daughter to see in London. He cured her of her stomach complaints, do you remember? And I was thinking that perhaps he might be able to help me."

Dorothy looked a bit dubious. "Yes, I remember," she replied slowly, "But that would necessitate traveling to London, and I honestly don't think you have the strength, milady."

"I could find the strength if there was the possibility of a cure," Lindsay said, with what she hoped was a small, brave smile. She reached out and grasped both of Dorothy's hands in her own. "Please, just ask Lady Marie for the name of the doctor, and then speak with Father. Please, Dorothy...I do so want to be well for my wedding."

This last part was so sappy that it almost made Lindsay gag, but it seemed to prove the point, and she only felt a little guilty about so shamelessly manipulating Dorothy, when she was so genuinely concerned.

Dorothy thought for a moment, then resolutely tucked Lindsay's bedclothes around her even more tightly. "I shall talk with both of them," she promised, bending to kiss Lin on the forehead, "And if necessary I shall take you to London myself." Lindsay cheered silently. Dorothy was now firmly convinced that this was the only thing to do, and Father would never be able to refuse her request in the face of such determination.

"Thank you so much, dear Dorothy," Lin murmured, as if half-asleep. Dorothy left the room quietly, and Lin silently congratulated herself on a terrific acting job. If only Mrs. Cummings could have seen her!

Lindsay spent the rest of the day chafing at her self-imposed confinement in bed, impatiently waiting for word from Dorothy. She appeared at dinnertime with a smile and a bowl of broth.

"It's all arranged, my pet," she said cheerily, "As soon as you are fit to travel, you and I will be going to London with a special escort of knights. A pity your father cannot go, or we could lodge at court, but we'll room at an inn and see that doctor, and he will cure whatever it is that ails you!"

Lindsay smiled back at her, all the while thinking that what really ailed her was not medical in nature and could be cured quite nicely by Arthur. With any luck, if things worked out, she wouldn't even visit the doctor at all. She didn't want to think about what his methods might include.

"Sit up and eat this, my love," Dorothy urged, helping Lindsay into a sitting position against the pillows, "Afterwards we shall spend a little time sitting by the fire. The sooner you are stronger, the sooner we can leave."

That will be very soon indeed, Lindsay happily, and then I will see Arthur again.

CHAPTER 26

If Lindsay had ever missed the conveniences of the twentieth century, it was during the torturously slow journey to London. By car it could have been accomplished in a day or so, but on horseback in the winter chill it took four days. Lindsay did refuse to ride in a litter. It looked like nothing more than a glorified stretcher, and she would die of embarrassment to be seen in it. She also didn't like the idea of being at the mercy of whoever carried it. What of they dropped her during a sudden attack? At least on horseback she had some control.

During those long, plodding days, Lindsay had time to perfect her strategy for seeing Arthur. As her father's daughter, she supposed that she could just waltz into court and ask to see him, but that sort of cold formality wasn't what she wanted at all. Something private and intimate would be better, and so Lindsay would have to send Arthur a message and arrange a special meeting.

Being only fifteen, and still operating under a set of rules that belonged to a world entirely different from Arthur's, Lindsay never stopped to think about how incredibly presumptuous it would be to ask a king to sneak out to a secret rendezvous. She had come a long way to be with him again, and she couldn't bear the thought of waiting for a more proper opportunity to see him, with both of their impending marriages hanging over their heads. Her plan was the only thing she could think of that might possibly work. As the little caravan at last reached the city and began wending its way through the busy streets to an inn at the heart of London, Lindsay felt confident that she would not be leaving the city again until she was Arthur's queen.

They settled into an inn, after much haggling between Dorothy and the proprietor. They arranged for a private room, but Dorothy would not allow Lindsay to step foot in it until she had thoroughly cleaned it. Then she insisted that Lin go straight to bed, to recover from the fatigue of the journey before visiting the doctor the next day.

Lindsay found it nearly impossible to sleep. The sounds of the city were enticing after the more rural surroundings of the castle. She was curious about being in a London much, much younger than the one she had once visited with her parents and sisters. The almost irresistible desire to go out and prowl the streets even took her mind off Arthur for a while. And then to realize that Arthur was so close after all the time she'd spent longing for him was equally unbearable.

But there were things to be arranged. As Dorothy came into the room, Lindsay said, "Dorothy, would you send Edgar to me with something warm to drink before I sleep?" Edgar was a page, eight years old, sent with them to relieve Dorothy of some of the little tasks necessary for their comfort, such as fetching, running errands, and shopping. He was a proud and polite little boy who liked Lindsay because she treated him as a brother. He would definitely have been an improvement over Giles.

Dorothy frowned. "Let me fetch you something myself, Lindsay," she fussed, twitching the bedclothes.

"Now Dorothy," Lindsay said reprovingly, "It's nearly dinnertime, and Father made you promise not to exhaust yourself over me. I would feel terrible if my illness also brought illness upon you. Enjoy your meal, and Edgar can bring up my drink."

Dorothy smiled. "Your Father did say that, didn't he? All right, milady. I'll send Edgar up to you shortly." She left the room quietly, wearing the soft smile that Sir Thomas' name always seemed to invoke.

Lindsay wondered, not for the first time, if there had once been something between them, but then Edgar entered the room with a steaming, fragrant mug. It was time to put her plan into action.

The little boy set the cup down next to the bed with exaggerated carefulness. Lindsay thanked him, and he rewarded her with a quick, shy smile. He had turned to leave before she called him back.

"Edgar," she said softly, with what she hoped was a weak but winning smile," I have a favor to ask of you. I need you to perform an errand for me."

Edgar shifted from one foot to the other, nervously. "Whatever you ask, milady," he said, trying to stand taller, "Your father told me to help in any way I could."

"Very well, then," Lindsay said, seriously. She reached under her pillow for an envelope that she had written and rewritten and finally sealed a few moments ago, and put it into the boy's hand.

"This is a very important message for King Arthur, which you must deliver to the castle and be sure he receives. Do you know the way there?"

"Oh, yes, milady" Edgar replied, with perfect assurance, "I have gone there many times with Sir Thomas."

"Good," Lindsay said, with a smile, "Then this should be easy for you. Just be sure that the king actually receives the message. You can even say that it is from Sir Thomas, and…" She reached for her purse on the table, and pulled out a coin, "…get yourself a treat on the way home." She had no qualms about lying to him. If Edgar said the message was from Sir Thomas, it would be certain to get Arthur's immediate attention.

Edgar's eyes grew very big as he looked at the coin in his palm, and Lindsay wondered just how much money she'd actually given him, since she couldn't even hope to understand medieval money. Edgar stammered his thanks and went off, promising to put the message into the king's own hand if possible. Lindsay settled back onto her pillows and prepared for a long wait until darkness fell.

Her note had been simple enough. In it, she greeted Arthur and then requested that he might meet her as he strolled in the castle gardens that evening, after the moon had risen and when most of the day's activity had ceased. It was a small thing to ask, and Lindsay got great satisfaction from enacting the scene in her head as she and Arthur reunited, pledged their mutual love, and were betrothed the next day. She conveniently overlooked the consequences: her father's wrath, Dorothy's disappointment, and the entire existence of Guinever. With her own personal romance movie playing so nicely in her imagination, Lindsay did drift off to sleep in the stuffy little inn room. She was confident that for once in her life, everything was going to work out the way it was supposed to.

CHAPTER 27

Lindsay didn't ask Arthur to reply to her note. She just assumed that they would meet in the castle gardens at dusk. If he didn't come...well, that was a possibility she refused to consider. She'd worked everything out perfectly and nothing would interfere with her plans now.

Lindsay pretended to awaken with great difficulty when Dorothy brought some broth for supper, and then feigned drowsiness after she'd eaten. Dorothy tucked her in, dimmed the light, and closed the door quietly behind her as she departed with the bowl and spoon. Lin forced herself to remain still beneath the covers, but she was almost breathless with excitement. Her stomach churned as she waited, but finally she was certain that Dorothy was safely downstairs. Lindsay crept out of bed and dressed as quickly as possible, hoping in the dimness that the gown she had chosen was at least somewhat attractive. Anyway, it would be dark where Arthur was, too, so he wouldn't be paying much attention to her appearance.

Downstairs in the inn's common dining room and bar, there was a great deal of noise and laughter, the perfect cover for Lindsay to sneak out through a back door into the alley. The heavy wooden door closed behind her, immediately muffling the sounds of the inn, and she stood in the filthy, mud-clogged street, trying to get her bearings.

This was the part that Lindsay dreaded. She was smart enough to realize that these streets were just as dangerous as New York City in her own time. She pulled the hood of her cloak over her face and made her way to the nearest main street, being careful to keep her head down and move quickly. At the same time, even though she was scared, she couldn't help but feel pleased at the romantic image she had of herself, bravely crossing the centuries to be reunited with her lost love. Straight out of a romance novel, but pleasing anyway.

Lindsay wondered how she could ever have considered the castle village to be dirty. It was a model of cleanliness compared to the mud and stench of those London streets. Lindsay had tried to pay attention to the surroundings when they first entered the city, but in the end she found her way to the palace simply by heading in the direction of the tallest towers and the most noise and activity. Every few minutes she would have to cower in a doorway when a boisterous group of men would spill out of a tavern, but barely a half-hour had passed by the time she came to the gates of Arthur's castle. There was a milling crowd of townspeople, messengers, and illicit women entertaining the guards. Hopefully it would be easy to slip in unnoticed, but Lindsay's stomach tightened with trepidation. What would she say if one of the guards did stop her? They would assume that she, too, was one of the street women, out at night without a man's protection.

She hovered around the periphery of the crowd, unable to take the last step necessary to reach Arthur. She put her fingers into the pocket of her cloak and felt for the photo of her family, now getting dog-eared from too much handling. Their faces were reassuring in the torchlight and gave her courage. This was it, the culmination of everything she'd been planning for months now. Taking a deep breath, Lindsay crept through the crowds and in the gates, unnoticed and unremarked.

As in Sir Robert's castle, the gardens were accessible from the castle courtyard. Lindsay found herself on a gravel path, surrounded by the scent of dry leaves and gardens now dormant for the winter. She shivered, even in her heavy woolen cloak, as the chill night air seemed to touch her for the first time. The noise and bustle of the streets seemed far behind her here.

The darkness was enclosing, despite the squares of light glowing from small windows set up high in the interior walls. Lindsay panicked a little. How would she ever find Arthur in this vast blackness, and why had she been so stupid as to suggest meeting here? She had her first misgivings: what if he didn't come? Maybe her summons had been a little silly and childish after all.

"Lindsay."

Her name was spoken quietly from somewhere to her left, and the quivering in her stomach suddenly invaded her arms and legs, turning into teeth-chattering chills that made walking calmly difficult to accomplish. Moving blindly, she almost tripped over a small stone bench and sat down on it quickly, with a distinct lack of grace.

Arthur carried a small lantern, and as Lindsay sat there, her eyes adjusted to its glow and she could see his face. Seeing him again, after all this time made Lin feel as if her bones had turned to mush. His face looked older and harsher, and his expression showed both weariness and a new maturity. Yet it was still the same face she had been treasuring in her memory, the same startling eyes and habitually unreadable scowl. The slightest encouragement would have made her throw herself into his arms, but something held her off.

"Hello, Arthur," Lindsay said softly, trying not to let her voice wobble, "I am so glad to see you again."

He continued to stare into the darkness as if he hadn't heard her, then said quietly, "I wasn't going to come here. It's ridiculous to skulk in the shadows like a knave. As king, I could receive you in the comfort of my home." He gestured at the dark bulk of the castle around them.

Lindsay was silent, not knowing what to say, and Arthur continued.

"I was sorry to hear from your father that you had not been well," he said politely, "Perhaps that is why I did come after all, out of surprise and concern that you should wish to meet me in this fashion when you are in such poor health. Surely the night air is not good for you."

Lindsay still didn't know how to respond. This conversation was not going at all like she had planned. After a moment she spoke, choosing her words carefully.

"I am sorry to have to arrange things in this way," she said, "I wanted to see you alone, and this was the only way I could think of."

"Skulking around in the dark," Arthur said bitterly, "How familiar. Shall I expect Giles in a moment, still protecting your virtue?"

Lindsay was stung by his tone. "I don't know where Giles is, and I don't care. I came here to see you, to tell you that I still love you and I've come back to be with you. Father and Giles can't touch you, now that you are king."

Arthur laughed ruefully. "I certainly wouldn't relish another tongue lashing like the one he gave me for trying to elope with you. I think it embarrasses him even now to think on it. But why is it you haven't come to me sooner, if this love burns so brightly? Was it first necessary that I should be king?"

"No!" Lindsay protested, with a sickening feeling. So he thought she was some sort of social climber. Frantically she tried again. "Arthur, if you only knew what I have gone through, to be with you again!"

"Tell me, then," he said, challengingly, "Tell me what you have gone through, and why I never heard from you again, even when I became king and we could have met properly."

Lindsay hung her head. "I can't tell you," she whispered. Even if she had told the truth, he wouldn't have believed her.

"Well, then," he said, with a trace of irony, "I don't think we have much more to discuss."

"I love you, Arthur," Lindsay whispered, miserably, "Don't you still love me?"

There was a dreadful silence, and then Arthur said, very gently, "No, Lindsay. And I don't know if I ever did. I cared about you, and enjoyed your company, but we barely had time to become friends, let alone find out if we loved. We were both too busy looking for a way out of situations we did not like."

Lindsay knew that in a few moments she would dissolve into a flood of tears. This she had never counted on, that he wouldn't want her anymore. The bottom was falling out of her carefully created world. She put her face into her hands.

She felt Arthur's hand touch her shoulder, and he gently coaxed her upright again. His voice became calm and soothing, oddly like that of Lin's father, and Lindsay suddenly had the strange feeling that he had become an adult while she remained a child.

"I'm sorry," he said, with a trace of the old Arthur, "I didn't intend to be cruel. It is only that so much has happened in my life since we were together. I am not the dissatisfied boy I was then. I am king of Britain, and its future is in my hands, and I hardly think of anything else. I barely have time to be a man, let alone a lover."

Silence again, until Lindsay said dully, "But you're going to marry that Guinever."

"Yes," Arthur replied, with a touch of warmth, "I wondered if you knew. Her father is an ally, and it is a good match. And we aren't without feelings for each other." He put this delicately, as if he was afraid of destroying a new and precious possession, and Lindsay didn't have the heart to tell him about what Guinever would do to him and his kingdom, even though she wanted to. With resignation, she knew that her battle was lost anyway, and Arthur would never be hers.

Feeling unbearably alone, Lindsay slowly stood up and straightened her skirts, trying to gather a little bit of pride around her again.

"I guess this is goodbye," she said softly, hoping her voice wasn't trembling too much.

"We will see each other again," Arthur said cheerfully, "It would please me greatly if you attended the wedding festivities, and with your father as one of my advisors, we will meet and hear news of each other often."

Lindsay shook her head. "No," she replied, "We won't ever see each other again." It would be too painful, she added silently.

Arthur had the grace not to pursue this. Instead he took both of her hands in his own. Lindsay gazed into his face one last time, at his still-startling eyes visible even in the dim light. His face had haunted her for months. How would she survive the future without him, while he still occupied her waking and sleeping thoughts?

The moment seemed to last for hours and then Arthur pulled her to him and kissed her, gently and lingeringly. Finally he released her and started to speak, but Lindsay thought she would die if he said one more word. She turned and fled.

Stumbling over hidden obstacles in the dark, and losing her way, it took Lindsay quite some time to reach the courtyard and the gates again. She stopped to compose herself and was about to pull her hood over her face again, before returning to the now-welcome anonymity of the street.

"Lady Lindsay?" A low, courteous voice spoke as a hand touched her elbow. It was a young man, dressed in the manner of a knight.

"I am Sir Gareth," he said, "My lord Arthur has asked that I escort you safely back to your lodgings."

Lindsay looked at him mutely, her eyes shining with tears, wondering how Arthur had managed to send him so quickly. Had he been privy to the entire conversation in the garden? She didn't even care anymore. She half turned and saw Arthur standing in the shadows of the garden path, and then she took Gareth's proffered arm and walked away. Her last image of Arthur, looking both handsome and sorrowful, burned behind her eyelids.

CHAPTER 28

Sir Gareth silently escorted Lindsay back to the inn. Somehow she made it back to her room undiscovered, then undressed and tried to put her gown back in the trunk in a way that wouldn't make Dorothy suspicious. Only then could she crawl under the covers and give in to miserable tears.

Arthur had made her feel like such a fool. It would almost have been better if he hadn't been so polite: at least then she could have gotten angry with him and salvaged a bit of her pride. As it was, she felt like some sort of idiot, running after a man who didn't want her at all. She had been so sure that they would end up in their own happily-ever-after.

Lindsay had to admit, however, that in some respects she and Arthur had grown very far apart. She was basically still a carefree teenager, and in her own world she was still quite far away from assuming all the adult responsibilities, but Arthur was a man and the king of all Britain. Perhaps neither of them was to blame if their love affair now seemed very childish and long ago to him.

Dorothy bustled in at the first light of dawn, after Lindsay had just a few fitful hours of sleep.

"Wake up, child," she said cheerily. Her tone made Lindsay want to strangle her, as she felt anything but cheerful herself, but Dorothy carried a bowl of steaming gruel and bullied Lindsay into eating it.

"You need nourishment," she said severely, "If anything, you look worse now than you did before we left. Eat up, girl, and then we need to dress you."

It was actually rather a relief to be manipulated, Lindsay thought, as Dorothy helped her put on a gown and her long concealing cloak. After all her planning, things had just screwed up anyway, so Lin was content to let someone else take care of her now.

The London streets weren't any less filthy or frightening by daylight. Dorothy took Lindsay's hand in the crook of her elbow and guided her along behind the broad backs of their bodyguards. The physician's establishment was just a few streets away, but Dorothy protected Lindsay as if they were traveling in the deepest forest. Lindsay thought wryly just how shocked she would be if she knew that her charge had been out wandering these same streets alone the previous night.

The physician's house was a dark timber and stucco dwelling in the middle of a row of closely packed houses. Dorothy led her up the steps where they were met by a servant and escorted inside. The interior was dark and had a musty, airless smell that made Lin wrinkle her nose in distaste. She began to wonder if being here was a very good idea. It was all very nice to just let Dorothy lead her around, but what was this so-called doctor going to do? Lindsay had to admit that she'd paid little attention to this part of the plan, assuming that she would have been with Arthur and so avoided the physician altogether.

The physician, Sanech, was a small, dark man with a sour expression, dressed in grubby velvet. Lindsay was somewhat relieved to see that his hands and fingernails were at least clean.

"This is the patient?" he said gruffly to Dorothy, eyeing Lindsay.

"Yes, milord," Dorothy replied. Sanech indicated a chair next to a long table covered with jars and dried herbs and mysterious substances. Lindsay sat down nervously, as Dorothy described the headaches to the physician.

"What star were you born under, milady?" the physician asked Lindsay suddenly.

Lindsay was taken aback. "Uh...I was born on the 4th of May," she said unhelpfully. What on earth could astrology possibly have to do with headaches? The physician, however, nodded sagely.

"I shall need a sample of the patient's urine," he announced, and Lindsay blushed bright red. This was going to be worse than she thought. Dorothy, however, produced a flask and handed it to him. Apparently she was well prepared. Lindsay had wondered that morning why Dorothy had suddenly taken to emptying the chamberpot, instead of the maids.

Sanech studied the contents of the flask for several minutes. Then he examined Lindsay by placing his fingers on each of her temples and the top of her head. She tried very hard not to shudder, reminding herself that his hands had at least appeared to be clean...

He asked Dorothy several questions about Lindsay's diet, the frequency of the headaches, and the phases of the moon when the pain was at its worse. Lindsay was beginning to get a bit irritated. They were her headaches, so why wasn't he asking her the questions? Finally he made his pronouncement.

"I believe the lady suffers from nerves, due to a congestion of the blood," he declared, "I shall make up a solution of root of peony mixed with oil of roses. Soak a linen cloth in this mixture and apply it to the pain. I also recommend a diet of barley water mixed with figs, honey, and licorice."

Well, that didn't sound too awful, Lindsay thought.

"If that doesn't lessen the pain," Sanech continued, "I will give you a mixture of herbs to take in a hot drink."

"Thank you," Dorothy said, taking several packets from him. She gave him several coins from her purse, then escorted Lindsay out of the house again.

"I'm surprised he didn't suggest blood-letting," Lindsay said flippantly, pulling her cloak more tightly around her.

"A common leech in the village can let blood," Dorothy replied scornfully, "If I thought it would help, I certainly wouldn't have had to bring you all the way to London. I am surprised, though, that he didn't prescribe the famed cure for most ailments."

"What's that?"

"The boiled down fat of a newly-deceased felon," Dorothy said, with great relish, "It's become quite popular."

"Ugh." Lindsay said feelingly, and then fell quiet.

When they reached the inn again, Dorothy made Lindsay return to bed and she was actually quite happy to. The feelings of depression and desolation were overtaking her again. She had lost Arthur, and she had sacrificed her real family and her real home for nothing.

Dorothy set about preparing the doctor's poultice. She boiled the peony and oil of roses and then spooned the fragrant concoction into a clean linen cloth, which she placed across Lin's temples.

"The physician said to apply this when the moon is in the favorable position," she explained, "If you are not cured by the time the moon phases change, then we shall try the herbal draught instead."

Lindsay was bemused by the idea that the phase of the moon had any effect on medicine, but she was too tired and depressed to really care very much. She closed her eyes, and a few tears trickled out.

"Lindsay," Dorothy said gently, sitting down on the bed and taking the girl's hand, "Perhaps it is time to talk about what is ailing your heart."

Lindsay opened her eyes and studied the woman's kind face. It no longer seemed important to deceive her.

"I have been to see Arthur," she said simply.

"Ah," Dorothy replied. "I was wondering when you would."

Lindsay was startled, and Dorothy actually grinned at her. "I'm a bit wiser than you think, my girl," she said." And I was suspicious when Edgar suddenly became so wealthy with pocket money. But I do hope,

Lindsay, that your entire illness has not been a deception in order to come to London."

"No," Lindsay said, sighing, "The headaches were...are...not a deception. They've become a bit less severe lately, so perhaps they would have cured themselves at home. Coming to London was mostly a ploy to see Arthur, I have to admit that, but I am still having headaches."

"Well then," Dorothy said, slightly mollified, "We will continue with the course of treatment, then."

They sat in silence for a few moments, then Dorothy spoke again.

"How did this meeting go, between yourself and King Arthur? I am certain that I would rather not know just when and where it took place."

"Probably not," Lin agreed, then to her mortification she burst into noisy tears. "It went miserably! Oh, Dorothy, there I was, telling him how much I loved him, and then he nicely but very firmly puts me off as if I was a mere doting child. I feel like such a fool. Am I so poor a judge of my own feelings, and his? He once said he loved me."

Lindsay expected comfort, but Dorothy was silent, staring into the flickering fire on the hearth with a half-melancholy, half-nostalgic expression.

"Let me tell you a tale, Lindsay," she said finally, "It concerns myself and your father, Sir Thomas. We grew up together, you know, and in time we made a natural progression from playmates to sharing deeper feelings for each other."

"You were in love?" Lindsay said, quietly, "You and my father?"

"Yes," she replied, with that small, private smile hovering around her lips again, "We were very much in love and we wanted to marry, but at that time your father was just a manservant in the castle, even though he was already a favorite of Sir Robert. My father was a merchant and he felt that I could make a better marriage." Even in the firelight, Lindsay could see that Dorothy's face was flushed with remembered outrage. "A better marriage! I was merely a merchant's daughter! But I bowed to my father's wishes and married another merchant, and Thomas went on to become seneschal and earn his knighthood."

"And yet you still love him."

"Yes. After all these years. There are times when I wish we had run off and married. Part of me wished for you to succeed in eloping with Arthur, for that very reason, which is why I carried your message to him even though I had an idea of what you had planned."

Somehow Lindsay wasn't surprised to discover that Dorothy had known all along.

"At least he continued to love you," she said morosely, "I can tell, now that I know the story. But Arthur moved beyond my reach."

Dorothy shook off her reverie and stood up. "Perhaps there were just too many differences between you and Arthur," she said, "Thomas and I grew up together, and we knew each other well. You and Arthur had barely met...perhaps given a little more time, you would have discovered that you weren't meant to be together at all. And becoming king certainly changes a man's outlook as well. He belongs to England, and even if he wanted to marry you now, he is betrothed to Guinever. Breaking that betrothal could create ill feelings between his kingdom and that of Guinever's father."

Lindsay nodded, but tears still sparkled in her eyes.

"Lindsay," Dorothy said, more gently, "All I can offer you is my sympathy, from also having given up the man I loved, and a little advice: hold on to your memories of the times you and Arthur shared, but let the rest go. Move ahead with your life. You've tried your best, but it was not meant to be. Best now to look forward."

Lin sighed and closed her eyes. The cloying sweetness of the poultice was now making her feel a bit nauseous. However, Dorothy's realism was oddly comforting. It was time to look ahead. Dorothy moved quietly around the room, stoking the fire and replacing the poultice with a fresh one. Lindsay felt tired and more peaceful.

Half asleep, she murmured, "Dorothy?"

"Yes?"

"I always felt that you were more of a mother to me than my own mother was. Now I know why."

Dorothy came over to the bed and kissed Lindsay's forehead. Lin could feel her smile against her skin.

"Sleep well, dear heart," Dorothy whispered. Then she dimmed the lamp and went quietly downstairs. Lindsay closed her eyes and drifted off to sleep.

CHAPTER 29

By the next morning Dorothy had begun making arrangements for their return home.

"Would you feel well enough to begin the journey this afternoon, my pet?" she asked Lindsay, with just a trace of irony. Apparently she still believed that Lin might be faking her illness, but Lindsay could have reassured her otherwise. She'd awoken with a wicked headache that assaulted her as soon as she'd opened her eyes.

"The smell of that peony and oil-of-whatever is making me sick to my stomach," she complained peevishly, as Dorothy set about making a new poultice.

"One more poultice and then we'll stop," Dorothy promised, "As your headache still seems to be with you, I'll make up this herbal draught, too." She boiled up another concoction from the physician's packets and gave it to Lindsay to drink. It was disgusting. One thing for sure, Lindsay promised herself, If I ever get home again I will never drink another cup of herbal tea for the rest of my life.

Whatever it was, though, it kept the worst of the headache at bay and made Lindsay pleasantly drowsy. She climbed on the back of her staid old mare one more time to begin the trip home, swaying a little in the beastly, uncomfortable sidesaddle that seemed to twist her spine into a new shape. Dorothy and Edgar mounted their horses and the escort moved around them, out of London and back into the countryside.

Lindsay rode with her eyes half closed, thinking with a depressed resignation about the rest of her life. Instead of being married to Arthur, a new great romantic heroine, she was probably going to spend the rest of her life married to that lump, Sir Cedric, and churning out babies until she was worn out. Castle life had suddenly lost its novelty, but Lindsay knew that she was stuck here, with this great echoing space in her head where the telepathy used to be.

Dorothy glanced at Lindsay and signaled for the party to halt and rest.

"Are you all right?" she asked Lindsay, with real concern. The girl was swaying in the saddle, very pale and sweaty. "Shall we make camp now?"

"No," Lindsay said, shaking off her drowsiness with great effort, "No, I want to go home. Let's move on."

Dorothy was clearly uncertain, but Lin moved her horse forward and they all plodded ahead on the road, which was just passing into the forest.

In this state, Lindsay felt just as she had on that first day, when she'd opened her eyes and found herself riding among a group like this in this same forest. Of course, in her actual time it was only a few months ago, but time here had become a very elusive quality and she felt like it had all happened years ago. How odd everyone had looked to her then, and how natural it was now to see Dorothy in her long skirts, cloak, and headdress, and Lin's own boots and long gown draped over the sidesaddle. She thought of the catty conversations between Mary and Alyce, and found it hard to believe that Alyce was now married and expecting a child. Probably Mary still hated her for presumably stealing Sir Cedric; that would be something else to look forward to, Mary's eternal acts of revenge. Dorothy mentioned that Mary had recently married a merchant and would have trouble adapting to the role of a shopkeeper's wife, so at odds with her own ideas about rank and position.

Lin rubbed her eyes, feeling overwhelmingly weary. If only she could fall asleep and find herself safely back in her own world again. Things had seemed so romantic and exotic here, when she had been with Arthur, but now it was just the same old thing. She had been the outcast, the unpopular one, at odds with her world until she had met him. That, at least, was something that she'd never had a chance at in her real life. Even if it had only lasted for a little while, she had loved Arthur and he had loved her, too. That precious time was something she'd have forever, just as Dorothy had said.

But there was something else she'd learned, too, about herself. She didn't have to be the same old Lindsay Hopkins who slunk through high school, a shadow trying to keep as low a profile as possible. She could be strong, and adventurous, and figure things out for herself, and find the kind of people she wanted to spend time with. Anyway, with the telepathy gone, there was nothing to hide anymore.

"If I ever get home again," she said aloud, part vow and part bargaining, "I will never be a wimp again."

"Lindsay?" Dorothy said, from beside her, "What did you say, child?"

Lindsay looked at her fuzzily. "Nothing." she whispered, then promptly fainted and fell off her horse. There was a sickening crunch as she landed full on her left arm.

Lindsay managed to break the bone in her forearm. Dorothy splinted it competently, and Lindsay rode the rest of the way home in a makeshift litter, but she was too foggy from pain and the herbal draughts to pay much attention.

After several more days of riding through the forest, the party arrived back at the castle. Lindsay awoke clear-headed the next morning. It would have been nice to find herself back home again, with the whole family clustered around her and Mom wiping her forehead with a cold cloth, but the now-familiar walls of her castle chamber were still there. Except for one notable difference: Aunt Sam was sitting beside her bed.

CHAPTER 30

Lindsay had never been so glad to see anyone in her whole life as she was to see Aunt Sam sitting there smiling at her. She wasn't even thinking about whether or not Sam could send her home again. She was just relieved to have her there, someone who knew everything about her and whom she wouldn't need to hide things from. Impulsively Lindsay leaned over to hug her aunt, forgetting all about her injured arm.

"Hey, take it easy," Samantha said, gently pushing her back against the pillows when Lindsay yelped in pain. "Thank goodness you chose an injury that medieval medical science has a pretty good grasp of!"

Lindsay looked down at her neatly sprinted arm for the first time. "Broken?" she asked.

Samantha nodded. "Nice and clean, luckily for you. From what Dorothy said, you landed right on it. Of course, you probably never would have fallen at all if you weren't drugged by all those herbal drinks. For heaven's sakes, Lindsay, don't you know what opium is?"

"Some kind of drug?" Lindsay said sheepishly.

"A very powerful, addictive drug," her aunt said sternly, "Thankfully, you only drank it for a few days, so you shouldn't have any trouble withdrawing from it. Did I mention, by the way, that sometimes these physicians use ground earthworms and other lovely stuff in their cures?"

"Ugh," Lindsay replied, as her stomach gave a nauseous flip, "But that's still better than rendered felon fat!"

Samantha looked startled for a moment, but then she laughed. "True," she admitted, "Well, other than your arm, it doesn't appear that any real damage occurred."

"Oh Aunt Sam," Lindsay sighed, happy just to gaze at her face, "I am so glad to see you."

"And I'm glad to see you," she responded, smoothing Lin's hair affectionately, "For a while there I was afraid that I wouldn't be able to get back here, or if I did, it would be too late and you'd be a worn-out drudge with scads of children."

Lindsay's smile drained away. "I really messed up, didn't I." she said softly.

"Yes," her aunt said, unequivocally, "You messed up in a big way. You didn't pay any attention to my warnings, and you're just damn lucky that I'm here now to put things to rights."

A faint hope surfaced in Lindsay's mind, even as her cheeks felt scalded and her eyes brimmed with easy tears at her aunt's words. Samantha's terseness was an indication of just how angry she had been at Lindsay, and Lin felt very meek.

"If it's any consolation," Lin said in a low voice, "I've paid for being so stupid."

"I know," Aunt Sam said, sighing, "And I could have predicted what would happen if you went waltzing back into Arthur's life now. I probably know him better than you do, after all my years of research."

"Maybe." Lindsay replied, stiffly, but she didn't for a moment believe that Samantha could know Arthur as well from all her books and manuscripts as Lin did from knowing and loving the real person, even just for a few days. But she certainly wasn't going to fight about it now, not when there were more pressing questions to ask.

"Aunt Sam, I'm sorry," Lin said, "I can only apologize so many times for being dumb. I lied to you, and I hurt Arthur, and Dorothy, and I'm honestly sorry."

Samantha studied her niece appraisingly, then her expression softened and she gave Lin a gentle hug.

"I guess I'll have to take your word for it," she said, "Although it's going to be a long time before I trust you again. I'm sure you have amply suffered the consequences, and now I'm just glad to see you again, almost all in one piece and not married, or deathly sick, or something."

"How did you get here?" Lin asked, at the same time noticing that her aunt didn't look terribly healthy herself. "The same way I did?"

"The same way," she conceded, "Although I have a bit more control over the process than you do, having had more practice and being a great deal stronger. But I was delayed at first, not knowing if you had actually succeeded in getting yourself back. Then your parents wanted to congratulate you after the show, so I was forced to lie and say that you were striking sets and would then go straight to the cast party. I had no idea how long you and I could be gone, with the time disparity, and the possibility that I might have to chase you down all over England."

"So they think I'm at the cast party?"

"Yes. And they think I'm there too, stepping in as a chaperone at the last minute. But fortunately here you are, not still in London with that dangerous quack doctor, or chasing around in search of Arthur, so you should arrive home before the party is even over."

So she was going home, Lin thought with incredible relief. But something was bothering her.

"You said 'you will arrive home', and not 'we'," Lin said slowly, "Aren't...aren't you coming home, too?"

Aunt Samantha got up from the bed and slowly paced around the room before answering.

"I've been thinking about this for a long time, Lin," she began thoughtfully, "I've been leading a double life for a long time now, and it's beginning to wear me down. I want to have a more stable life, in just one place and time, instead of constantly shifting back and forth until my head spins. I love Garrick with all my heart and I would be quite miserable without him. Perhaps I've always belonged in this place, and that's why I was so drawn to it in my career. This is where I want to be, Lin, in a home with him for the rest of my life."

"But Aunt Sam!" Lin cried, scrambling awkwardly out of bed, "How can you just leave your other life behind? What about your work? You could be a world-renowned scholar, with the fame you'd earn from proving that King Arthur actually existed!"

"And how would I prove it?" she scoffed, "By standing up at a conference full of staid old professors and claiming that I had personally met Arthur when my niece tried to elope with him?" She laughed. "They'd rip me to shreds!"

Lindsay laughed a little at that image, but her eyes were filling with tears again.

"Lindsay." Aunt Sam put her hands on Lin's shoulders and looked into her eyes. "That life just doesn't seem very important to me anymore. My life is here. I had more difficulty making the transition this time than I ever have before, and I probably can't continue to do it much longer. I have to make a choice, and this is it."

Lindsay looked back at her with tears spilling down her cheeks. "You aren't forced to stay here because of me, are you?" she asked, in a small voice.

"No," Samantha replied firmly, smiling at Lin, "I could get us both back if I really wanted to, but I feel weaker and my capabilities are just about at an end. Just the way yours ended when you came here on your own and overreached your abilities."

"I know," Lin said wistfully, "I can't read you, or anyone else, now. I never thought I'd miss the telepathy business, but I do." She wiped her eyes on the back of her good hand, and tried to be calm. "So what do I tell everyone when they finally figure out that you're not coming back?"

"Well," Samantha said, with a sigh, "I've left a note in your things...you can tell your parents that I gave it to you. It says that I'm tired of my old life and I'm going away, I can't handle the pressure anymore. You can back me up by saying that I'd told you I was unhappy and troubled."

"Seems sort of inconclusive," Lin commented.

"Well, I haven't the heart to leave a suicide note," Samantha said ruefully, "And this will leave my options open in case I ever do have to come back."

Lindsay sighed, and leaned against her aunt's shoulder. "When do I go home?"

"Right away. But there is one more thing I want to tell you."

"What?"

Samantha smiled shyly. "I'm going to have a baby."

Lindsay's tears spilled over again, and she hugged her aunt awkwardly. "Oh, Aunt Sam! And I won't ever see him, or her...But I'm happy for you. Happy and sad."

Samantha returned the hug. "Somehow I think you'll know what it is, when the time comes. It will filter through, after all that's been between us, even if you did blast most of your sensitivity away. But now it's time to send you home. Do you have something for a talisman?"

Lin reached into the bodice of her gown and produced the photo of her family, now sadly frayed and torn. "This," she said, showing it to her aunt.

"That will do nicely," Samantha said, "Now stand in the center of the room. I'm afraid I'll have to take the splint off your arm, because I don't know if it will travel. And don't forget, when you get back you'll need to concoct a story about how you broke your arm, and have them take you to the emergency room. I can assure you that physical conditions stay with you."

She gently untied the bandages that kept the splint in place, but Lin still grimaced in pain. She had to hug the arm to her stomach to keep it still.

"Do you want me to tap my heels together three times so that the ruby slippers will work?" she said flippantly, trying to keep the wobble out of her voice. Aunt Sam just smiled, and stood before Lindsay, loosely grasping her good hand, which also held the photo.

"Ready?" she said.

"Aunt Sam..." Lin's voice trailed off and she swallowed hard. "I just want you to know...I'll miss you terribly. I can never thank you enough for everything. I love you."

Samantha smiled tremulously, and Lin realized that this was even more difficult for her. "I love you too, Lin." she said huskily, "And if it's a girl, I'll be naming her after you." Then she kissed Lin and disentangled herself again, except for the one hand.

"Goodbye," she said, with a smile, "Have a good life, Lin."

Lindsay just had time to wish her the same when the room started to swim before her eyes, just as it had so long ago on the school stage. The grayness rose around her like a fog, and her last image of Aunt Samantha was of her standing tall and beautiful, with closed eyes and a slight smile, willing Lin back home.

Then the mist cleared and Lindsay found herself back in the prop room, teeth chattering, holding her arm awkwardly. She closed her eyes for a moment, sniffing the familiar smell of canvas and paint and sweat, then she left the stage and headed for the cafeteria, where she could hear the cast party still in full swing. Taking a deep breath, she plunged into the noise and lights and went to find Kathi.

CHAPTER 31

It would have been nice if Lindsay came back home and suddenly became irresistible to every boy in school, and the new Miss Popularity, but of course it didn't work that way. She did enjoy a few days of celebrity status when the word got around that she had broken her arm when a piece of scenery fell on it, but she had bravely carried on until the next day when she finally went to the emergency room. It was a good story, not as good as what really happened, of course, but still pretty good. It cemented her friendship with all the drama club techies, and Lindsay found that she had a new group of people to hang out with, people that she felt comfortable with and didn't need to pretend with.

Chris was still cool, and Lindsay regretfully admitted that, while they were still friends in a say-hi-when-passing-in-the-hall fashion, their best friends days were over. It would never be the same, but Lindsay was pretty sure she wouldn't want it to be, anyway. Chris was born to be one of the popular girls, and Lindsay didn't have much to say to her now.

Late at night, Lindsay would curl up in the armchair by the fireplace in the kitchen, and think about everyone in the castle. As time went on, it was easier to toss the whole thing off as a dream, but she knew it hadn't been. It was too real, even now. And Aunt Sam was gone, just as she said she would be. Lin's mom had gone crazy trying to find her for months, until she finally accepted the fact that Samantha didn't want to be found, wherever she was. Lin had trouble keeping the secret to herself, and several times she almost told her mother, just to keep her from worrying. But her mom wouldn't have believed her anyway, and then she would have worried about Lindsay' mental health on top of everything else, so Lin kept her mouth shut. I would have been nice, though, to tell her mom that Samantha wa happy with her husband and baby daughter.

Lin thought of Arthur often, probably too often since she still didn' have a boyfriend. Oddly enough, sometimes she wished that she coulc have met him without realizing what he was destined to be, and jus have loved him for himself. It would have been nice to save him from the heartache of Guinever's unfaithfulness, but Aunt Sam was right ultimately the time-travel secret would have been revealed, anc Camelot would never have been the same. And perhaps Lindsay woulc have been quickly disillusioned about what it really meant to be a queen, but part of her still dreamed about being Arthur's wife.

It was strange, too, how much she missed being able to read people' thoughts, however vaguely. The ability never came back. Perhaps she hac just burned it out when she went back to Arthur, and fried those partic- ular brain cells beyond repair. Or perhaps she was only meant to have it in order to go to the castle, and once the experience was over she nc longer needed the telepathy. Still, sometimes she felt empty without it.

It was another beautiful fall day, and once again Lindsay left the bus stop and took her time walking home. It was weird not to have Kath around this year, now that she was off at college, but it was fun being a junior, and having a bunch of friends, instead of spending her days slinking around invisibly.

The door banged with its familiar sound as she went into the kitchen but Mom was already home.

"Hi, Lin," she called from the pantry, "There's a big stack of college catalogs for you with today's mail."

Lindsay tossed her books down and leafed through the glossy folders with their nearly identical pictures of students siting around grassy green lawns with their professors. She had already decided that she would go to school to major in medieval history, just like Aunt Sam. Perhaps she could take over the research her aunt had begun into the Arthurian legends...after all, what could be more satisfying than to prove what she already knew: that Arthur had been a flesh-and-blood man, and Camelot a real place.

"Of course, you'll need to do junior year abroad, at least," a voice said suddenly, inside her head, "University College in London, I think. I'll even tell you where to find my research notes."

Lindsay looked startled for a moment, but then she just smiled.

THE END